# A SHADOW OF MYSELF

PETER FLAMM, whose real name was Erich Mosse (1891–1963), was born to a Jewish family in Berlin. He began writing columns and short stories for the newspapers belonging to his uncle, Rudolf Mosse, while still a medical student. *A Shadow of Myself* was his debut novel, and it met with huge acclaim when it was first published in 1926. In the following years, he published three further novels while continuing to practise as a doctor until he was forced to flee Germany in 1933. He settled in New York and worked as a psychiatrist and psychoanalyst, treating William Faulkner, among others.

SIMON PARE is a translator from French and German who lives near Zurich. His translation of *The Flying Mountain* by Christoph Ransmayr was longlisted for the International Booker Prize, and he was part of the team that translated Angela Merkel's political memoirs, *Freedom*, into English.

RACHEL SEIFFERT is a novelist. Her books include *The Dark Room* (2001), shortlisted for the Man Booker Prize; *A Boy in Winter* (2017), shortlisted for the Women's Prize for Fiction; and, most recently, *Once the Deed is Done* (2025). In 2003, she was named one of *Granta*'s Best of Young British Novelists; in 2011, she received the E. M. Forster Award from the American Academy of Arts and Letters; and in 2025, she was elected a Fellow of the Royal Society of Literature.

# A SHADOW OF MYSELF

## Peter Flamm

Translated from the German
by Simon Pare

With an Introduction
by Rachel Seiffert

PUSHKIN PRESS

Pushkin Press
Somerset House, Strand
London WC2R 1LA

Originally published as "Ich?" by Peter Flamm
First published by S. Fischer in 1926
© S. Fischer Verlag GmbH, Frankfurt am Main 2023
English translation © 2025 Simon Pare

First published by Pushkin Press in 2025

ISBN 13: 978-1-80533-226-8

All rights reserved. No part of this publication may be reproduced, stored in a retrieval system or transmitted in any form or by any means, electronic, mechanical, photocopying, recording or otherwise, without prior permission in writing from Pushkin Press

A CIP catalogue record for this title is available from the British Library

The authorised representative in the EEA is
eucomply OÜ, Pärnu mnt. 139b-14, 11317, Tallinn, Estonia,
hello@eucompliancepartner.com, +33757690241

The translation of this book was supported by
a grant from the Goethe-Institut.

Designed and typeset by Tetragon, London
Printed and bound in the United Kingdom by Clays Ltd, Elcograf S.p.A.

Pushkin Press is committed to a sustainable future for our business, our readers and our planet. This book is made from paper from forests that support responsible forestry.

www.pushkinpress.com

1 3 5 7 9 8 6 4 2

# CONTENTS

*Introduction by Rachel Seiffert*
—7—

A SHADOW OF MYSELF
—13—

LOOKING BACK
—141—

# INTRODUCTION

Congratulations. You have in your hands a rare masterpiece. Rediscovered in the S. Fischer archives almost a century after its first publication and sixty years after its author's passing, this novel made Peter Flamm's name when it was released in 1926, lauded for its modernist flair and terrifying vision of post-war alienation.

A *Heimkehrroman*—a tale of a returning soldier—it falls within a venerable German storytelling tradition. This reissue sees Flamm take his place alongside other twentieth-century masters of the art, from Wolfgang Borchert to Heinrich Böll and Erich Maria Remarque, all of whose writing also recalls the folk tales of collective memory gathered together in the Grimm collection; stories of soldiers of fortune, returning from unnamed battles of old with nothing but their boots and their haversacks. *A Shadow of Myself* makes a great companion piece to *Berlin, Alexanderplatz*, too. Alfred Döblin was a contemporary of Flamm's; they share a formal inventiveness, a dizzying narrative directness, and a sharp-eyed perspective on their times. In Döblin's book, the returner is a prisoner rather

## INTRODUCTION

than a soldier, but both novels capture Weimar Germany in all its contradictions.

Before we go any further, though, I should issue a warning. This book will make demands of you. To read it, you must be able to bear its many uncertainties.

Framed as a confession, the narrator tells us from the outset that all is not right here. 'It is not me, your honours, but a dead man speaking through my lips.' The novel's first sentence sets out its unnerving premise: the dual identity of its protagonist. On the last day of war, he says, hearing news of the revolution in Berlin and Munich, he went stumbling out across the blasted landscape of Verdun, across 'abandoned graves, abandoned ground, the abandoned dead.' He'd survived the slaughter, but couldn't trust in the promise of change. 'A future? We'd work, we'd need to start again from scratch, where are the white sheets, we'll be at the front in the muck again with the generals in the rear, the generals are always in the rear, those rich people driving cars, with all the glory, the grub and the women, while the others croak...'

But then there, under the ruins of Douaumont, he chanced upon a fallen compatriot in the mud. 'My hand patted down his body, I didn't mean to, it just happened automatically [...] my heart beating like mad, but over the pounding I felt, with a strange, ecstatic thrill, the small grey booklet, the passport I'd taken from the dead man, his passport, his name—and his destiny.'

INTRODUCTION

The man speaking claims to be Wilhelm Bettuch, a baker and member of the Frankfurt proletariat. The man he speaks through—the man whose destiny he claims to have stolen from the grave—is Hans Stern, a surgeon and Berlin bourgeois. Flamm's swap is audacious: a logical impossibility and a literary sleight of hand, dissolving personal and class boundaries at a stroke. Bettuch may doubt in the revolution which ended the fighting, but he seems to have been afforded a personal revolution of his own.

Leaving the trenches, he slips into the life of a Berlin doctor: Stern's comfortable apartment, his surgeon's practice, his marriage to the beautiful Grete. 'Now I have hatched out, now I'm someone else, I have a different name, I'm a different person—it's so easy, you only need to change your clothing, names maketh the man, and now I'm a doctor, Dr Hans Stern, yes, that's who I am, me, I'm an educated person, I'm rich, my worries are over.'

Except in the midst of this good fortune, Bettuch finds himself plagued by doubts and questions. At the same time as loving Grete, he feels he is cheating his wife of the truth. 'The secret has been placed like a barrier over my mouth, over happiness, pleasure and life.' To make matters worse, an old associate comes calling and our protagonist discovers this Sven Borges has designs on Grete—perhaps she has even been unfaithful. And then a further visitor, Frau Bussy Sandor, turns out to be his own lover, and Bettuch/Stern must confront the fact that he is equally faithless.

INTRODUCTION

This trading places conceit would be enough for many a novel. Showing the reader Stern's life through Bettuch's incredulous eyes, Flamm reveals the German middle classes as duplicitous, their respectability nothing more than a confidence trick. However, Flamm doesn't rest there—and this is where the novel's genius lies. His narrator may insist he is Bettuch living as another, yet the reader can never be certain that such a swap has taken place at all.

For all his dislocation, his unnerved sense that he is living as another, our narrator is Stern to all those around him. From the moment he arrives, he is on familiar ground. 'I'd never been to Berlin, but I knew this was Berlin and I was stunned.' Leaving the station, he's greeted by a man who clearly knows him, delighted to welcome the doctor home again. Out on afternoon walks with Grete, he receives nods from neighbours and patients: 'See, no one's forgotten you.' When he doesn't acknowledge Bussy, she reacts just as a lover would: hurt and spurned. It is only the dog, Nero, which raises our suspicions: by turns hostile and frightened, the animal cannot settle around his old master—but still he follows him everywhere. So is he Wilhelm Bettuch, a baker living a lie, or is he Hans Stern, a surgeon with a shattered mind?

With his new life one of feverish exhaustion, of fathomless contradiction, the narrator seeks stability in routine, opening his surgery, seeing his patients; the day of his return becomes a year, time proving as slippery in this novel as identity. And all the while, 'my words tumble out of my mouth on their own, my blood finds its path of its own choosing, around me are muscles and flesh, I'm sitting inside myself looking out of my eyes as if through a narrow shaft: there is the world, there is everything else, people and streets and clouds and a room and destinies.'

Who am I if my experiences have made me a stranger even to myself? This is the novel's fundamental question, its fundamental uncertainty. 'How am I supposed to relate this with a tongue not mine in a mouth not mine? How are you supposed to believe me when I don't even believe myself?' This nervous intensity drives Flamm's prose, its headlong first-person narration; it permeates the novel's structure, too, scenes and events tumbling over one another. On every page, Flamm pushes at limits—not least when he has Stern's life cross over with the Bettuch family's, leaving their fate placed in his deeply uncertain hands.

But I shan't say more on that; I shall let you read on and discover for yourself how this plays out.

I will close, though, with a note on the author, and an encouragement to read the postscript—an elegant, reflective piece, also by Flamm but written decades after the novel's publication, and long after he had left Germany.

Born Erich Mosse in Berlin in 1891, his father a high court judge and city elder, his uncle the founder of the *Berliner Tageblatt*, his family deeply invested in German culture, he says of himself, 'I was born a Jew, but I felt more German than many other Germans. I spoke German, I wrote German, I felt

## INTRODUCTION

German.' It was only later, in adulthood and exile, that he came to see his family's many achievements and plaudits as 'a giant, many-layered plaster on a wound I didn't want to see'.

Readers who, like me, feel the absence of German Jewish life in the novel – who assume, for example, that Hans Stern may be Jewish because of his surname yet find this neither confirmed nor denied, and who are then also left wondering at the absence of antisemitism in a novel written by a Jewish German during the rise of the Nazis – will find the postscript enlightening, if painful.

How to understand home when home is gone? Flamm tackles this question head on. He left writing behind when he left Germany; he made a new life in New York, and began a new career as an analyst. Germany's (and literature's) loss were America's (and psychoanalysis's) gain, and aspects of this second chapter in life are described with enviable lightness and insight. But loss is also there, of course, a restless companion.

> Maybe I cannot afford to live hand in hand with the past. It was too painful, and the hand was too easily paralysed. I forget what I wish to forget. I have called this a constructive and healthy neurosis. We cannot carry all our ballast around with us all the time. We throw what bothers us overboard—as far as possible.

*—Rachel Seiffert, 2025*

# A SHADOW OF MYSELF

It is not me, your honours, but a dead man speaking through my lips. It's not me standing here, not my arm raised, not my hair that has turned white, not of my doing, none of my doing.

You won't understand. You think this must be a living person, this is a human being speaking—or a madman. I'm not mad, I just don't know. But I've been lying in the ground for ten years, my limbs rotted, my bones grey powder, my breath… I have no breath. It's all silent. It's all over. I'm lying in the ground near Verdun. Up above are the ruins of Douaumont, the wind's blowing across abandoned graves, abandoned ground, the abandoned dead. Go there, dig into the sand, burrow away in the large shell crater to the left with water in it, maybe soft mud. Don't be afraid—the war's over, no shell will fall and splatter you to bits, no screams ring out now, no limbs fly through the air, no blood, no shredded bodies. It's quiet. Not a sound. For evermore. Now you bend down. You scrape away a bit of earth. And you find… me. Yes, bones and skull and dust and my name which is not my name and yet is, my destiny that belongs not to me but to someone else, though it has now befallen me, every bit as suffocating as my own.

How am I supposed to relate this with a tongue not mine in a mouth not mine? How are you supposed to believe me when I don't even believe myself? But that's how it was, that's what happened, it was real, it was a day like many others—no, not like many others, because Lieutenant Basch told us there was a revolution, a revolution in Munich and Berlin, the war was over, after four years it was over, no more shells, no death, no mud, no obligation, no laws, no shrapnel, no pressure: everything seemed to be dissolving, falling apart. A new era, a new life.

I was drunk, we were all drunk. Something was singing inside me, surging up inside me, so I climbed out of the trench, my senses reeling—there was no way it could be over so suddenly, we'd been waiting for so long that we'd given up believing it would ever end. Now, a new opening, a new life, we wouldn't lie around in muck any more, we'd be back in a room on white sheets, we'd have a future. A future? We'd work, we'd need to start again from scratch, where are the white sheets, we'll be at the front in the muck again with the generals in the rear, the generals are always in the rear, those rich guys driving cars, stealing all the glory, the grub and the women, while the others croak, while we...

I clambered out of the dugout, tripped over mounds and holes, stumbled over corpses and tree trunks; it was a cold night, the moon was shining, music trickling from the dugout, fever boiling my blood, I was so tired I could have toppled over and yet I was driven, driven forwards, driven on by fear... suddenly something was lying in front of me, a dark mass, I almost fell over it. I made to walk on, back to the dugout... why was I out here anyway instead of with my comrades, singing with them, celebrating, what had lured me out here in the middle of the night, alone among wrecked carts and collapsed walls, alone among... the dead? Yes, it was a dead man, I knew, obviously, he'd gone out on patrol yesterday, twenty-four hours before the end, the war was over, and he'd been killed a day before, even the final bullet struck a mother, couldn't we have stopped a day earlier, so stupid, now he was dead, lying there, the doctor, an 'educated' man, though what good was his education to him now, he was only a sergeant like me, ought to have been a lieutenant... now he was dead, and I... My hand patted down his body. I didn't mean to, it just happened automatically, I'd walked here automatically—had I meant to, had I known? Automatically. How? My trembling hand groped its way over the body, mud, sticky blood, I turned on my torch, its small, blunt beam creeping spookily through the shadows; then two eyes were staring up at me, dead empty eyes twinkling between sunken lids, I recoiled, my hand was shaking... wasn't the head nodding, wasn't there a mischievous grin on those cold, blue lips? I was lost; back in the dugout I clutched my hands to my chest, my heart beating like mad, but over the pounding I felt, with a strange, ecstatic thrill, the small grey booklet, the passport I'd taken from the dead man, his passport, his name—and his destiny.

I didn't know at the time. No one asked you amid the hurrahs for the revolution, who asks for papers, who checks them, who knows a name? We're all human, we're all brothers, and the other guy was dead, he didn't care, rotting in the mud with twinkling eyes, bones and dust, eugh!

I was sitting on the train, an express train, first class of course, how easy it is to get used to, how strange too that all the agitation was gone, quite natural the whole thing. Did I use to stand by the oven door and get up in the middle of the night? And the dough was risen and hard, and through the door the embers caught you right in the face, singed your skin, and young Hennings burnt his apron and one hand and screamed so loud... no way, no way, that wasn't me, that isn't me, I was on this train, an elegant, educated man, a rich man reclining on a red-cushioned seat, first class, of course you can pity the others packed into fourth class like animals, like cattle, unable to even sit down and so tired, their knees shaking, but they have to stand, all of them, even the small, thin dragoon, pale-faced beneath his black parted hair, who stared and stared at me earlier with so much pain in his eyes until suddenly he fell over, all white in the face. Or did I only dream it or see a picture once, and it's a memory of something that may or may not be real?

'When you reach Berlin,' says the fat baldie on the cushioned seat opposite. 'Revolution—who'd have believed it! You *are* going to Berlin?'

'Is this train going to Berlin? It is? Yes. I actually meant to... Of course I'm going to Berlin.'

Of course? Why *did* I go? I didn't mean to, but I was sucked there. I thought it was my choice, but how then could I forget my mother and my sister in Frankfurt, how could I? Hadn't seen them for a year, but all the same—Berlin now? Berlin, of course. It wasn't even difficult, it wasn't even an issue. I smiled, I had to smile the whole time, but there was still a darkness on my soul, a strange, hovering shadow, heavy and smothering.

Outside in the corridor a man was leaning against the window, watching the landscape flash past. I couldn't see his face, but his narrow back, his slanted shoulders, the left pulled higher than the right, and the curious tension in his neck all seemed familiar; something came bubbling up inside me, a peculiar agitation, an unprecedented hatred, an almost physical revulsion. I couldn't take my eyes off him. Was I hypnotized? I was travelling first class and I knew no one here! Why should I hate a stranger, a neck, a back, with such pointless, unprovoked hatred? What was he to me?

Now the back turned, the neck creased with diagonal folds, now the head turned into profile—a stranger. But I knew him: all the blood came rushing to my forehead, there was a darkness there that scared me, it was like a blow to the head, my thoughts became confused, I wanted to stand up, turn away; but the man had noticed me now and swivelled his body abruptly in my direction, a pair of eyes stared hard and fierce until the whites looked as if they might pop out, the nostrils began to quake, the hand started to clench into a fist, for a second it looked as if the fist was going to rise and punch the narrow, thin pane of glass between our faces—then with a jolt he lowered it, turned away contemptuously and disappeared with rapid, spasmodic movements.

I sat there numb. What was that? Had I dreamt it? Was I hallucinating? The war had certainly affected my nerves, no wonder, but it would probably pass. When I'd settled down and gone back to work... I wiped my brow with my hand. Strange, how white my hand was, thin and transparent, thin blue veins marbling the wax-like skin, as if it weren't my hand, as if...

Strange, the thought crossed my mind, what kind of person am I, what am I actually, sitting here, and what weird hands I have!

The train pulled into the station. I'd never been to Berlin, but I knew this was Berlin and I was stunned. I walked along the platform, down the station steps and turned left along Königgrätzer Strasse to Potsdamer Platz. In Bellevuestrasse a man came towards me, was about to pass, gave a start, stopped and greeted me, and there was a sparkle in his eye and then a rejoicing hand tugging at my arm.

'Gosh, it's you, doctor, you're here, you're alive? How's Grete going to react? A rumour something had happened to you… you did send her a telegram? I was at her house only yesterday and your mother happened to be there too. They were all very worried. And your last letter was so strange, deathly premonitions, my God, no one should write such things, and then that rumour, and now you're here, how wonderful, I'll walk a stretch with you if you like, of course, come on, a car, how can you walk so slowly, and wasn't there anyone to meet you at the station?'

I sat in the car, next to a stranger driving me I didn't know where. I couldn't think straight, I was not at all surprised, everything was happening automatically, I was floating on a river, on a cool, silvery surface, there'd been a war and now there was peace, I was walking through the crowd and then along comes a man and drives me in a car. Isn't that natural? Everything's natural. We all get one lucky break, you just have to seize it, and the miracle lasts only until it becomes reality.

The car pulled into the street and stopped. The throbbing of the engine suddenly ceased and a strange silence enveloped my brain, I got out mechanically, watched unthinking as the other man counted, scanned the house, the row of windows, a particular one, suddenly my heart stood still, the ground seemed to tilt and the world began to spin before my eyes in green and gold circles. But her image was always before me, standing up there at the window—who? A woman, girlish in appearance, shining golden-brown Titian locks above a face turned pale, a face full of sweetness, fear, pain, longing and so much love—who was this meant for, whose are this woman and this love, who possessed her: I'd give my whole life... no, I don't want to move, why's he pushing me towards the door, I want to stay standing here looking up for ever... the stairs, where am I supposed to... why's my heart hammering like this?

My God, a door opened, up on the second floor, there were sixty-two steps, why did I count them, count them for no reason, the door swung open, it was already ajar, an old woman standing there in a white bonnet with trembling hands, and then, appearing from the narrow hallway, in the draughty air, in the flickering white light... suddenly the girl was there, the woman from the window, standing there palely and smiling with a faint, sickly, modest smile, a small, pallid, twitching mouth, her shining eyes blue and gazing radiantly into mine until a shudder ran through her slender limbs, her eyes sank behind long, dark lashes, and her suddenly waxen body began to sway. She'd have fallen, but one leap and I was by her side, she was lying in my arms, her pallid lips moving quietly, her warm breath brushing my face and I shook as I held that warm body in my embrace, then she raised her thin hand as if in a dream, touched my hair disbelievingly, tentatively, the lashes slowly rising, a blue beam of indescribable tenderness shining forth from her eyes and, as tear after tear trickled unstoppably over those cheeks, the lips opened moist and soft for an inseparable kiss.

How long did we stand there? I was oblivious to time, oblivious to the world, noticing only something tugging at my leg, it kept coming, jumping up and falling back while something hot scorched my leg, a hot, tingling, piercing pain. I wouldn't even have noticed it but for her scream and her horrified face, her forehead flushed red again; suddenly her hands were no longer above me, her wide-open eyes were staring sideways now and I felt as if I were in some terrible danger, as if I had to wrench myself back to my senses with all my might, wake up, defend myself, but I was gripped by such confusion, intoxicated by the smell of her hair and the scent of her skin and all I kept seeing was her face, there was no one there, I wasn't really here, it was all a dream, happiness seemingly hanging in the air, that was real, I mustn't wake up, I had to stay very quiet… what was screaming, why were the lips pulling away, they'd just touched me, they'd just kissed me, what's twitching, why's this face grimacing, what's happening, what's tearing at me?!

Two dog's eyes spurting green flames, a black shaggy body, a wild shaggy head, bared white teeth sunk and caught in my flesh, and blood flowing, my blood trickling hot and sticky towards my foot, down my sock, a small dark stain there on the rug, a strange red mass, the man by the door shouting, his heavy hand plunging into the animal's coat, hauling it backwards; again it charges forwards, he kicks it in the nose and at last it lets go, its jowls flap, its red tongue hangs out bloodied and powerless, sheepishly it creeps away to the wall, growling, eyes still on me, eyes still on me...

'How could you, Frau Grete,' the man's panting voice says, 'a fine welcome! That beast is mad, it could've torn him apart. It might be rabid. And why don't *you* defend yourself? Look at the slobber flying from its jaws, how it's looking and staring at you, like a... like a human being.'

'That has never happened before, never,' she shudders helplessly, then suddenly, 'Hans, Hans, you're back, out of the blue you're back, my God, I'm going out of my mind, that animal's crazy, it bit you, why did it bite you—don't just stand there, go and fetch a doctor, you can see it's bleeding.'

'Nothing serious, forget it,' the man says. 'A bit of gauze, a plaster, you must have some here—'

'Oh yes.' And she goes off and comes back and the trouser leg is rolled up and the wound's bandaged, they take off my coat without asking, why should they ask, don't I belong here, isn't this my building, my room, my flat, my... wife?! My wife! This girl, these hands, lips, hair, these eyes—my wife!! This is mad, what's going on, this can't be happening. Who is this? I'm in a stranger's home. I don't know anyone. Who is she? What's her name? Who do these people think I am? It's a misunderstanding. Who am I? Who am I??

'You must get some rest,' she says then, and her voice slices like a ray of light through all the dark clouds. 'You shouldn't think or tell us anything, just sleep now. There's enough time. The war's over and you are here with me. Everything's all right now, isn't it? Oh Hans…'

What can I say to her? I have no idea, I don't understand it myself. It's too much at once. I've done something, but I can't remember what. And I'm tired. I want to sleep. Everything's all right, isn't it? Everything's all right.

I'm lying on the couch. My leg's hurting. I've shut my eyes. When I half open them, the dog is over there, huddled up in the corner, growling away, sucking in air through its raised muzzle, peering over at me. I'd love to sleep, but there's an agitation in me, a dull hammering inside my skull, and I feel very alone. My brain's in a peculiar state. For no reason I count the yellow and black squares on the wallpaper, then the black ones separately—there are 136 of them—I can feel my body lying on the couch, I'm sitting inside my body and feel it lying there, hands on the blanket, my backside on the soft fabric, my brain swimming in my skull, my muscles streaked with white nerves and brown veins. Who am I?

My hand glides over my chest, moving back and forth as if in a mechanical caress. Something crackles. In the left pocket, to the left of my chest something curls forward, feels furry. This one touch sets my heart pounding, suddenly a catch is sprung in my brain, an abrupt crack rends the wall: the passport!

How could I forget? Where have I been? Such fog, such ghostly twilight! Here in my pocket, a stranger's passport.

Stolen: no matter. A defenceless corpse: no harm done. He's no poorer for it, but I am richer. What's in a name! Have I not suffered enough from mine? 'Bettuch, Wilhelm Bettuch?' Is that a name? A person's name? Bedcloth? At school, out in the playground, they would stand around me, pulling at my trousers, my jacket, my shirt. Bettuch, you cloth! Like in the fairy tale, lay the table yourself! Did you sleep well? Give us a wave! We'll beat the crumbs off you! You've got stains all over! We'll put you in our pockets! Handkerchief, pillow case!

Bettuch! What kind of father, what kind of ancestor would wear that name quietly! Let it wear him down without protesting! Without casting the yoke from his neck! A person bears no blame for the name he wears... 'What's your name?' 'Bedcloth.' He smiles. Who? Everyone. People. The whole world. Twist their lips into a crooked smile. How do you take someone like that seriously, trust him, give him a title, a job, a position? Shouldn't I have made master baker long ago? Did someone take me on as an apprentice? Of course. But there was another less skilled man, who'd always been less skilled, and I was passed over. Always passed over. Blonde Liesel at the dancehall: looked at me with blue eyes, tilted her neck very gently towards me during the waltz, her little curls brushing my right cheek lovingly and affectionately, I led her hot and breathless back to her seat, her mother is there, 'Bettuch,' I say with a bow, 'Wilhelm Bettuch!' At this Liesel turns red, her small, dark lips become pinched, a giggle tickling her throat, always the same giggle, it's everywhere, it murders everything, a momentary lustre dulls, a burgeoning warmth freezes and recedes, and I stand there alone.

A name, a word: what does it have to do with me? What's a man and his name? How can you even name a person as you would a thing, name a life that's evolving and always changing? He who was free is now caught in a net from birth—labelled, marked! Always bowed, so what use is strength; always tamed, so what use wildness, courage and work. Now I have hatched, now I'm someone else, I have a different name, I'm a different person—it's so easy, you only need to change your clothing, names maketh the man, and now I'm a doctor, Dr Hans Stern, yes, that's who I am, me, I'm an educated person, I'm rich, my worries are over, what is a corpse, I took his good fortune!

Over there the dog has got up from its corner and is prowling around the room, its head cocked, its eyes glowing green. After each lap of the room it stops at the end of the couch, draws itself up, looks at me, places its paws on the heavy carpet, lowers its head and begins to whimper in a long, torturous wail.

What's wrong with this mutt? Everyone's good to me, everyone loves me, strangers put me in a car, strange arms drape themselves around my neck, strange hands tremble as they stroke my face. This animal alone is nasty, hates me, tears the flesh from my leg, drawing blood, glowers at me, wild and testy, a gloomy, skulking foe.

You must try to win it over, it's a good animal. Usually it's good, so why not now? You have to be nice to it, stroke it. Come here, Nero! How do I know its name? Nero? Yes, here it comes, yes, it's pricked up its ears, the bushes above its eyebrows begin to twitch strangely, its head goes up, its tail wags, beating, lashing around, suddenly it jumps up onto the divan, I'm so startled I rear up, but its head is next to mine, its soft, damp tongue next to my cheek, and now its tongue is running over my ears, over my cheeks, chin and hands. The animal is beside itself, out of control, its whimpering turns to a bark, its snarl cuts violently through the air, it jumps up from the divan and back down again, spins around as if out of its wits, writhes on the floor, runs over to the table, the wardrobe, the window, its whole body quivering, now it's back beside me, sucking in the air, sniffing at my shoe, along my trouser legs, at the bandage; the barking stops, more pitiful, horrible whining; it lies down flat on the ground, on the floor, on the cold, desolate floorboards. Its tongue hangs out as it pants, its nostrils are dark red, foam gathering on its muzzle. 'Nero,' I call in a totally unfamiliar voice, jump off the divan in one leap to stroke it, dig my hand into its coat, my head warm next to its head... but the movement stops in mid-air, I see the dog in the mirror, I see the objects in the room, the chair by the table, the books on it, the ashtray, the lamp, I see the animal on the floor... and a stranger beside it, dark hair covering his forehead, head bent over the animal's coat, the hand... rooted to the spot,

I look up, the other man also raises his face, two eyes stare at me and, horrified, I let go of the animal, so does the other man... what's this, I feel dizzy, the other man turns pale too, lurches upright as I do, leaps towards the mirror, I glance around, so does he: no one, there's no one in the room but me, I'm all alone, only the image in the mirror, and that... is me, myself, it's the only possibility, I'm all alone, I'm lonely, terribly alone, I tap my whole body, arms and face, one hand stroking the other: me, me, me, someone else is me, I'm someone else, the dead man who's now alive, face and body changed, muscles, flesh, guts, brain and soul. Not me? No longer mine? I no longer me? What sees with my eyes, what is touched by my hands, my thoughts, my own thoughts... no longer mine?

Breathless horror grips me. I try to think, but everything is frozen, an icy silence inside my skull as a fearful, alabaster face stares out of the mirror. Suddenly there's a twitch, a searing flush courses through me, the hand pats the breast pocket again automatically, now everything is clear: the passport, the other man's name, the name caused all of this, they are mystically connected, face and name indissociable, and now I am the other man and must live out his death, live his life while he lies out there under the ground, in the mud, and I step into his life as if through a picture frame; but I know everything, I stand on the other side like a spectator, I'm still myself and watch myself being the other man and at the same time myself, a man behind his image.

A calm has come over me now, a strange quietness. Everything is empty, I have no more fear, it was perhaps too much, I'm tired, you can only cope with so much, an instant can never be fully captured, you can only understand things in the light of the past, which is a good thing because otherwise the soul would shatter. A shield, a bulwark against yourself, against insanity, excess and madness; everything's fine, the past totally extinguished, no more war or work; I can't remember how things used to be, not that it matters anyway, I'm a new person, a new life is beginning, a new future. Now, now is happiness, now, when I step through that door, beyond lies happiness, beyond lies...

The door opens, slowly and cautiously, a narrow gap, a head squeezes through it, auburn hair glows in the sunlight, a white hand rests on the handle, large, blue, fearful eyes listen out: here she is next to me, her breath touches my face... no, no, no.

'What's wrong, you're looking at me strangely, why did you flinch?'

'Nothing, oh, I didn't mean anything by it, I was just startled, I'm not used to any of this yet, your being... here, I was alone in the trenches for so long, among men, shelling all the time, noise all the time, orders all the time and being ready to die, and now all of a sudden... there's someone here with me, a woman, so beautiful—'

'My foolish darling, now I'm blushing,' and she holds my eyes closed.

Should I tell her? Must I not tell her?

'Just look what a sight I am, my hair, my face, it's all—'

I get no further: she's holding me in her arms, she's clinging to me, I'm so weak, I can't help being weak, can't help loving her, that's right, I saw her face and right away fell in love with her and lacked the strength to tell her I wasn't him, that her kisses were intended for someone else, loved someone else, another man, another man!

'Come through now, you've slept enough, the sun will set soon, the table is laid and has been for some time, everything will be cold, and Mother is waiting, Mother is there too, I couldn't stand it so I told her you're here but no one else; today you need some peace and quiet first, tomorrow is a different matter, your friends will insist on coming: Bobby has already sent his servant round three times, it was nice of him to bring you straight here in the car; Bussy Sandor sent that big bunch of lilacs with a pink note; I'm telling it all wrong but you mustn't get angry, and imagine this, Sven Borges has just got back too, I haven't seen him in all this time, he only had leave once and was very forward, I'll tell you about it later, and now half an hour ago, while you were lying in there, the telephone rings... strange, isn't it? He must have come on the same train as you.'

The back, the sloping shoulders—was that him? He must be the man on the train. The darkness is back, Sven Borges, again I feel a pane of glass before my eyes, it should've been smashed, but it's unbreakable, unbreakable...

It carries straight on, there's no time to think, it's like a children's book, one new page after another, one surprise after another, but it's my own life. I'm in the next room, a table has been set with fine white damask and crystal glasses standing on it, green and red goblets, flowers placed here and there, small violets, in the middle a large, tall vase full of glowing, open roses, right and left two candelabras with nine white candles, so festive, and she's taken my hand like a child, just as Mother would lead me in by my hand on my birthday, surprises, presents; there's a hunched old woman there, her sparse white hair sticking up wildly around the old, crumpled forehead, the thin, pursed lips twitching, her still, grey eyes behind the golden spectacles peering at me, large and astonished; now she bangs her stick on the floor, comes step by step towards me, the spectacles slide off her pointed nose, the stick clatters to the floor, the small, parched arms coil around my neck while the small, ancient body is wracked with sobs and happiness.

'Mother...'

Tears well up in my eyes, I don't know why. This is my mother. I'm seized by a great longing, a nameless ache, I want to fall at her feet, but I'm stopped by something heavy and dry squatting in my throat, musty and suffocating.

Now we're sitting at the table, the lights flicker, there's not much talk, the old servant carries in the dishes, white china, thin and translucent with a red dragon pattern, and over there on the right-hand wall hangs a picture, it must be

Grete and a young man next to her in uniform; she must have noticed my gaze because her eyes also swivel that way, there's a smile on her face, she has her hand on mine, withdraws it mischievously.

Throwing back her head, she says, 'Actually, you look a bit shabby in civilian clothes, you know. Remember when we had our first photograph taken together, Father and Mother had no idea about our engagement, and I was so proud of your uniform. You were just serving until it was time for your appointment and the official announcement and you would have to take it off again; we went there, your moustache, you used to brush up your black bristles, thank God *that's* gone, so war is good for something after all, that stupid tickling, and you looked picture-postcard handsome, I was a stupid girl, I liked it back then, look'—and she jumps up and back with the picture in her hand amid a burst of bright laughter—'your eyes were like saucers, like a marzipan prince, and those silver braids, one of them tore off during our hurried parting that evening when you wanted one last kiss and it snagged on the chair arm, and I hurriedly sewed it back on again, and the sergeant noticed and asked, but you wouldn't admit anything and preferred to be detained instead, no, you were a stalwart toy soldier, you could never shake off that name, my little toy soldier, and now you're a big one and have had enough of it and I have had enough of it too, it's better like this, even in civvies, it really is.'

She's serious now and pensive, her fine, slender fingers playing with the silver knife rest, I turn half towards her, her face in profile, her white neck bent over the picture, a gentle and moving silhouette; suddenly all her cheerfulness is gone and with a pained, strangely weary and careworn expression around her lips she whispers:

'A piece of our life is gone, the war took it from us, cheated us of our life together, where is it now? When you're married, you have to build a life together or what's the point! How often I sat here and pined for you and wondered what you were doing out there, were you in a trench, maybe chatting with comrades, drinking, maybe with my picture in your hand telling the others about us, was your mind in this room here or somewhere else entirely, over by enemy lines, studying their positions, or a captain was standing there or an attack just starting, and I sat here unable to move, it was all taking place without me while I sat here powerless, as if I were blind, bullets flying, blood spurting in all directions, arms and legs flying, this one's guts hanging out, that one's brains, just after you'd been chatting to them; it was horrific to sit here on my own and Mother always silent and never any news; sometimes I thought I didn't know if you were even still alive, whether you might not already be in the ground, long since a shapeless mass, and then suddenly I had this feeling of being married to a dead man without even knowing it, and then I could have screamed, my own life sitting here, this body sitting on this chair, then it was over, such a horrible chill rising up inside, like a cold fever; sometimes I sat for hours and couldn't stand up, in bed at night I couldn't sleep, I saw you lying beside me on the white sheet, your forehead completely white, it was half dream, half madness, blood on your hair, and time resting on it like a doll, yes, the time I was living through, that you were living through... a strangely stiff doll, squatting on the centre of my chest, drawing out my breath with a soundless breath, almost choking me.'

'Grete, Grete, my child, you...' For the first time the name has come out of my mouth, it's no longer so bizarre, I've just taken her hand and am holding it in mine, she's all cold and shivering, her face very pale, I run my hand over her hair, again and again, I have no thoughts, her chest rises and falls, a tear runs down her cheek, hot and slow, I stand up, I take her in my arms, I kiss away her tears, silent, excruciating sobs shake her body, I don't let go of her; eventually she calms down, a smile flickers on her lips again, she pulls herself together violently, takes her white tissue, vigorously wipes her eyes, laughing again now and mocking how I'm looking at her, sits down at the table again, stabs her fork into the meat, cuts off a large chunk, dips it into the gravy, pushes it into my mouth and says, 'Well, this is more important than anything else. I'm a stupid, hysterical thing, and now we won't mention it again, all right?'

No, we don't mention it again. But she's pale, her mouth is laughing, she talks incessantly, she jokes and begins a thousand anecdotes, but I know she isn't with me, only her mouth is laughing, her eye is still large, grave and shocked, and behind that white forehead a small soul lies sick and bleeding from a thousand cuts.

The meal is finished, we've got up from the table, and the old maid clears away the plates; Mother, who has sat chewing away in silence so far, mumbling half-intelligible things to herself, has now taken her stick, hobbles around the table, puts her arm through mine, points with a near-triumphant expression to the door on the left; I look quizzically at Grete, there's a sweet Madonna-like smile on her face, a delicate, happy flush briefly lights up her cheeks.

'He's in there sleeping,' she beams, 'but he can wake up now. It's not every day he has a new father come home.'

God on the cross who bears the sins of the world: a wave has caught me and swept me along and won't let me go, impossible to go back, impossible to undo what has been done, the coast slips away, and out into the dizzying sea I go, out of my depth... everything is ablaze before my eyes.

The small room is all white, pink and blue walls, white blankets, white fabric, the windows are open and the wind billows the feathery white curtains into the room, round spots of sunshine dappling the yellow straw mat; it's completely quiet, I can hear my breath as the two women stand beside me, and in the corner is a small bed, white lacquered wood, white pillows; three steps and she's there, leaning over the frame, the wood pressing into her lap, her dress riding up; I see her black shoes, the white stockings, two round calves, and her body rebounds as if on springs, she exhales deeply and in her hands something moves, small, sleep-dazed movements, stretching, waking up and growing strong and kicking the blanket off its little tucked-up legs. A delicate, tiny body squirms naked and red in her arms, flailing his limbs at the light, at life and the world, little fists clenched to the point of pain, eyelids screwed up tight. Now she's next to me, holding out the child in front of her like a priest presenting the host, passing him into my arms. I look down now, not daring to move. 'Your boy, isn't he now,' she says. 'Looks just like you, black hair and the little round nose—I found some pictures of you as a boy in the desk, wearing shorts, pretty, funny little pictures—see he can't help laughing along, and his tiny hands are reaching for your fingers, yes-o-yes-o-yes, Daddy's back, Daddy's here, say Da-dee, Da-dee, look, he's already pouting his little lips, Da-dee, there, did you hear that, his first word, I've taught him it so often and now he's got it, today's the first time he's said it, Da-dee, Da-dee, my consolation, my little creature!'

There's a scraping at the door, a low growling and snuffling, the handle jerks down twice and suddenly the dog is in the room, racing towards me in a few great, wild bounds, jumping up with both paws at the child, making me almost drop him, but Grete rips him out of my hands at the last minute, and the animal's rage subsides; it fixes its big, red, flaming eyes on me, leaps around the room, barking absurdly, and back to the woman, rubs itself against her knee with a whimper, its tail waving suppliantly, its tongue dangling out of its open mouth, and it turns its bushy head, looks up at her beseechingly and is now up on its hind legs, braced against her arm that is clinging on to the child, and breathlessly it licks up and down her arms, the little legs and the child's naked body.

'Have you gone mad, Nero? What on earth is wrong with you? I nearly dropped him!'

'Get that animal out of here,' I say quietly, 'I don't want to see it,' and I walk out of the door and back into my room.

I feel very sick. The animal has flustered me. It'll haunt my dreams. It's like a human being. But what does it want? What has an animal got to do with any of this? Ridiculous. I'm imagining everything. My nerves are completely shot. The bloody war. But everything's fine now: I have a house, I have... a wife, I have a... kid; I didn't want this, I didn't mean this when I took the passport, I just wanted to get out of that mud, all I wanted was to start a new life, I'm not a proletarian, I'm a gentleman now, I truly am, so I'm not deceiving anyone, she can be quite content with me because otherwise she'd have no one and the child would say 'Daddy' into thin air, the same way it smiles, with its little, red legs; why does the animal bother me: it should watch out, I'm not going to give up any of this, I'm here now and I'll defend it all tooth and nail, my child, my wife... Grete! It's terrible! I'm cheating her, I've never seen a woman like her before, I'm cheating on her with myself; it's all so grim, but I love her,

I do, I love her, that's how quickly it can happen, it's such a new feeling when I think of her, something right here in my chest that aches, her hair, her lips, her eyes when she looks at you, the way she leant over the child, what am I doing, what the hell am I doing?

There's a knock. It's her. How could I leave her to come and be alone in my room. It's the behaviour of a proletarian, not an educated person. Why am I afraid to open the door? Because I love her? Am I a thief? I'm going crazy!

'I apologize,' she says, 'for that stupid animal! But how could I know? Maybe you should actually lie here for a while on your own and get some rest, you're not used to people. You need to rest, but let me be with you at least; you shut your eyes, I want to be completely quiet and just be able to look at you, no more than that, at least look at you, is that all right?'

'Put your hand on my forehead,' I say very quietly and close my eyes.

'Yes, that's good, you're my second child now! In my arms for evermore!'

How long have I been lying here like this? Her hand on my forehead, always her hand! I am her child, I'm safe, the storm has carried me here to these hands, everything's all right.

Am I asleep? I'd like to speak if I could, tell this hand everything as it rests slender and quiet and trusting on my hot face. I'll never be able to speak again, the secret has been placed like a barrier over my mouth, over happiness, pleasure and life. But that's why I did it, that's exactly why! I want to live, I want to be free to kiss these slender fingers, my lips between these slender fingers, over their cool round tips, the small smooth pink nails.

'What are you doing?' she said, confused. 'You're meant to be sleeping!'

'I am, I am, I'm sleeping. It's all a dream, all a dream, Grete, it doesn't matter, we're not allowed to wonder if it's really happening, but you're happy, aren't you, as happy as I am, you love me and we're together, I'm holding your finger, your hand, the rest is ghosts and demons trying to hurl us down into the darkness, but you are the light, you make me good, I shed all of that, I want to be good to you, nothing can stop me, you're my wife, my saviour, and I love you, I love you, Grete!'

Her lips are on mine, I kiss her forehead, chest, neck and eyes, her chest heaves, her eyes are large, soft and dark, her hands completely powerless, we lie together on the divan, her breath comes hot and excited on my face, I feel her body trembling... There's a voice outside, words on the other side of the door, a commotion somewhere, I must have heard it somewhere before, it's like a stab, I don't want to know, it's nothing to do with me, she's in my arms, the world stops here, at the wall, I know nothing beyond, I can't face knowing anything else...

There's a very timid knock, and through the wall the old maid's voice says, 'Herr Sven Borges is here. He would like to pay his respects to the doctor and his wife.'

She has got up—evening has come, and a stale light clings to the windowpane—I can't see her eyes any more, her forehead is angled downwards and her usually soft chin thrusts out hard and black into the half-light.

'We won't receive him,' she says after a long silence, her voice emotionless and strangely hoarse, her arms and legs tense.

'Does he love you?'

'I don't know. Maybe he hates me too. It doesn't matter. I don't like him.' Suddenly turning: 'He was here, on leave, six months ago, then again three months ago, bearing greetings from you, an afternoon like today; he sat on the chair opposite me, his gaze constantly meeting mine, he has grey, round eyes like cold bullets, you can't shake off his stare, like a rat's. He'd seen you, been with you, I was happy to hear a little about you, invited him to dinner—why not, he's your friend—you were far away in the trenches and now there was a little of you in the room, very close to me, he'd observed your most recent facial expressions, your words, had seen you laughing, seen you moving, some of that must be reflected, must have been absorbed by him, I was so glad, I wasn't alone any more, I heard his words without knowing what they were, you'd heard his voice too, it was like walking on a bridge, floating over the endlessly wide river of time, across the many miles of land between us, and I was with you, saw you in the flesh before me, it was all there again.

'He didn't understand though, thought my cheerfulness was on his account, the joy and bliss on my face intended for him, he held my hands, I still hadn't caught on, then suddenly his lips were on them, a burning heat ran up my arms, I jerked back, looked at him in shock, his hands groping the air, his lips stammering something unintelligible, for two seconds only, then he was in control of himself again, a mean smile on his lips and a dull glint in his eyes, he bowed and was gone.'

'The second time?'

'Three months later he was back. Why did he get leave and never you? I was furious with you, hurt, did you love me less than he did, maybe I felt pity for him or it was vanity or curiosity or simply because he had some relation to you. I let him in again, he seemed to have aged: there were strange furrows on his brow, his left shoulder was hunched up, his face was grey. "Will the war be over soon?" I asked. "Don't you want it to be?" he replied, his voice hollow-sounding, his lips pressed tightly together; he didn't seem to be there when he spoke, as if occupied by something else entirely. I asked after you, he was evasive, I put my hand on his, and he looked at me, as helpless as an animal, and a green light came into his eyes, the furrows on his white brow rose as one and he suddenly shouted, "I won't leave you, I won't rest until I know everything, I'm on his trail, I'm on his trail."'

'When? Where? What a madman!'

'Yes, I think so too. His lips were white as chalk, his shoulders sloping upwards, and I couldn't utter a word, couldn't ask him anything or respond at all. He didn't even seem to expect me to, and in the doorway he turned around one last time, the tension in his face was gone, his features slack, full of pain and poverty. "Forgive me," he whispered, almost sobbing, "forgive me. Everything I've said, everything I'm going to do is more powerful than me, it's beyond anyone, it'll be the death of me, I know, but of him too, him too, before me, first!"'

'But that's—'

'Don't let him in, I'm scared.'

'Of what? Of what? This is ridiculous.'

I spoke some very brave words, blood boiling in my temples, I'd got up and was standing in front of her; something was creeping up on me, he had to be faced down, what trail was he on, what might he know, what kind of person could know anything about it, and if he did, he'd be dealt with, no problem, I was the other man now, nothing could happen, neither to me nor to Grete. On my trail? Impossible. Never. Could I have guessed that it wasn't that at all, that there was another trail, something completely different I had no idea about?

I'd put my arm around her waist: I was completely certain now, I had a mission, a responsibility to protect her from everything, she was weak and she put herself in my custody; I was her husband, there were no more ghosts, I had every right, she was reliant on me, she was in need and I was the man to save her, I was very happy, pride coursed through me, a sense of power I had never felt before, I didn't need to look up to her, she looked up at me instead, she in her weakness and me in my power, who would dare to disturb my happiness?

In the doorway she stops once more, wraps one arm passionately around my neck, presses her trembling body against mine, 'Don't go, don't go,' she whispers, and I feel a defiance inside me, verging on rage, a feeling I've never had before: is she rebelling against me, is it possible she loves the other guy, does she? I could hit her, I could raise my arm to her, punch her in the face, slap those white cheeks, that white, transparent skin, that soft, round neck until blood pours out; she's my creature, she lives within me, through me alone, I am her husband and her master, so why is she looking at another man? Resisting? Resisting? How dare she!

'What's that look in your eye?' she says, her face very close, her eyes staring helplessly and entreatingly into mine, 'I thought it was all over long ago, that you'd have forgotten it out there?'

Forgotten what?

I stare at her; I can't work out where that came from. Hitting? This face? This body? This creature gifted to me, entrusted to me, honouring me, blessing me: Grete, Grete!

'Never again, all right? I belong to you and you alone, you know that now and for ever. All the longing of these years always for you, all my hope, all my fear, all my despair always for you, all my love and all my life, you and you always, always you, always you!'

I kiss her on the forehead, on the eyes and the mouth, she smiles, she is besotted and happy, I could fall at her feet now, kiss her feet, those slender legs as she leant over the baby, my child from her womb, my child, I love everything about her, every eyelash, every little hair, and now her head's resting on my chest, my hand over her hair, she stands up straight, she smiles, nothing can happen now, 'Come,' she says, and we enter, arm in arm.

Inside, the lights are already on, electric lights; the curtains are drawn across the windows, six empty chairs stand around the table in the centre, the desk to the left is wide and brown with heavy white writing paper on it, rectangular like a gravestone, in front of it an open book, what's in it, who's read it, maybe I did too? My desk, and it all comes back to me... I used to sit here, of course, I worked here once, but what kind of work; this chair at the desk with the round rush seat... it turns, around and around, I'd like to sit on it now or rest my hand on it and spin it around, with the central spindle silvery and thin and absurdly tall, the seat like a wide, flat head on top of a skinny neck, and then it hurtles to the final twist and with a crash it flies off, and the neck is all battered and crooked, and now I put it back on again, all crooked, and it spirals back down, all skewed and drunken until it can go no further and the wood groans and the edge of the seat disc is rammed in at a slant. Standing bolt upright by the left-hand door is Sven Borges, his shoulders no longer twitching but resting calm and level, his neck straight; he looks at Grete, steps forward and bows, an engaging smile playing around his lips; he bends over her hand and kisses it, takes a step towards me and stretches out his hand to me too, grabbing mine coarsely, his hand as wide as a mountain range and anything that stumbles into it is crushed, so I make my grip like iron and there's a sort of battle between our hands; 'Oh, let go again,' Grete says with a laugh, her voice a little hoarse, her face a little tormented, 'I'm glad that your first visit is to Hans and me together, now you're both here and both alive, the war is over, and your evil premonitions have evaporated into nothing!'

She wants to appear cheerful and light-hearted; there's no more heaviness, no more danger, I'm with her and I won't let anything touch her, she senses this, it's good that I'm here, for you shouldn't leave a woman like her alone, and with the way he's looking at her I could hurl myself at him, but it's as if there's a wall between us, like the glass pane on the train.

Now we're sitting at the table and Grete has asked for liqueur to be served, in a small, cut-glass carafe and small, coloured glasses, why go to these lengths for him, we should grab him by the collar and throw him out, cast him out like a viper, and why's he silent the whole time, saying nothing, just sitting there—'another drop'—'by all means'—she says this like a mole, a fish, sucking on tight with a thousand suckers;

we have to lure him out of his reserve, not beat around the bush, not sneak around like him, what can he know, who is he, didn't he already do something to me once before Grete was around, before she was around, was there some time like this before, I feel as if I'm lying in my grave, I've seen this all before and I've no idea how, something comes flying through the air and crashes into you, soundless and white the soul swims through the air, everything's like jelly, impalpable and hazy: into the centre of this world you are dropped, full of wonder, and I'm sitting here in a tasteful room and opposite me is a man who hates me, I don't know why, and there's Grete, my wife, and I'm like an actor on a stage, will I know my lines, has the writer finished my part, he definitely will in time, and I simply parrot it, something age-old, my words tumble out of my mouth on their own, my blood finds a path of its own choosing, around me are muscles and flesh, I'm sitting inside myself looking out of my eyes as if through a narrow shaft: there is the world, there is everything else, people and streets and clouds and a room and destinies, and I belong with them, in there… where am I, something has to happen, I've got to do something, otherwise it'll happen to me; I must listen to what the other two are saying, it's essential I do; why's Grete standing up—I should call her back—going out with small, light, dancing footsteps, what? so he'll see it; what? she's handing me over to him, betraying me to him, she loves him, she does love him, I want to go after her, I have to; have to throw myself at her and on top of her, what do

I care about this man, she's my wife, I want to go after her, but deal with him first, yes, him first, I'm going to get hold of him, I'm going to grab him by the throat…

Then he looks at me suddenly, his eyes cold and piercing, and says, 'Your wife has left the room so I'm going to seize this chance to have a word with you; let's forget what came between us and please forgive my behaviour on the train today, I caught sight of you so suddenly; Captain Koch told me you'd been killed on the last day, I couldn't believe it and went through the trenches one more time because, as you know, my post wasn't far from yours, in fact we should have visited each other more often, but that's all in the past, and if I really had found your corpse, I'd have laid a wreath of roses, maybe, I'd have forgotten everything, because death drowns out everything, but now you're alive, now you're back home, back home with your wife, and I want to be friends again.'

My friend? Roses? His eyes are cold and grey, his face is hard, his neck thin and hunched, his lips pressed together, a twitch in his shoulder: he's holding off, he has time, he's toying with his prey.

Something has happened once before, he's sat opposite me like this once before, I don't know when and I don't know why, it was much like now, but that doesn't matter now, he wants to be my friend, he mustn't feel too rejected, the war is over, everything's fine, we must be grateful to be alive, not to be lying dead somewhere, shredded in the mud; I'm all alone, we need a friend and why shouldn't it be him, I don't know anyone else, I can't remember knowing anyone at all, he's smart and I'm not scared, no one should think I am—oh no, neither him nor Grete—I'm a man and I've proved it, I dared to do what nobody else dares to do and I'm alive, it's all going to start over now, it's just the beginning, it won't be easy and he should help me, I want to let him in on my plans, ask him what the job market's like now, he must know because after all his job… and mine…

'Are you going to start work straight away?' I hear from the other side of the table like an echo.

'Yes, I mean in a few days, maybe, we have to see first, it's possible that this or that needs sorting out first so that… have to rest a bit first, right, that's what you're doing too, you're not taking on a full load right away, we have to wait and see how things pan out.'

'Why wait? Get in there before the others turn up. Now everyone is streaming back into the professions, the competition's hotting up, and if we don't make hay now, it'll soon be too late.'

He wants to reel me in, he wants to lure me out, I'm going to give myself away, I won't let him prove anything, he's sniffing around, nose to the trail, I've no problem with that, I'm as sharp as he is, I'm as educated as he is, a friend, a friend probing for information, or I'm just prickly and he means well, sure, where's Grete, I need to be ready just in case, no, I have to strike, no, I have to strike first, attack the flank, just in case.

'What about you? How about your profession?'
'Starts tomorrow. There are always criminals!'
'A sorry profession...'
'You think so? Wearing the wig, being a prosecutor, punishing injustice on behalf of a higher power...'
'It will prevail regardless.'
'But it depends on the agency of our hands. Humans need protecting from themselves. You didn't talk like this before.'

Before? Is he coming for me again? Who's he threatening? From one foxhole to the next—I don't want him to find me.

'That was before the war, before war and death. We're all different now, parts of our selves have been snuffed out and changed.'

'But there are things that time does not erase, they endure and remain visible to the initiated as a bloody mark until they are atoned for.'

'Maybe.'

'And if the law doesn't punish them, there are wounds that never heal and just keep opening, again and again. Because there's something stuck inside them, a tiny piece of shrapnel. But it can never heal, the pus keeps seeping through the delicate skin. As a doctor you are best placed to realize that.'

Me, as a doctor, me, yes of course, what, me a doctor, but he... why's he telling me this, why's he giving that away, so stupid, so incredibly stupid, I know I'm a doctor, a surgeon, of course I do, there must be instruments in the cupboard next door, the door on the right leads to the surgery, it's all white, and the instruments are gleaming, steam is rising from a gas cooker behind the glass partition and there are test tubes, the sterilizer, the glass jars with the fitted lids, cotton swabs and powder and iodine, all of that is clear, it's just as if there were a fog around my brain and now it's lifting, I have to go in there right away, I have to see everything, touch it, check everything's in the right place, not broken, not dusty, Grete's not allowed in, I banned her once, so who's been taking care of it, must ask, must hire a nurse and a guard, got to get everything up and running again, start all over again, the patients are standing darkly in the waiting room, he must excuse me, I really can't sit here chatting any longer, that's not what my life's like, I've got to work, earn money, lots of money, I must buy Grete a ring, with a black pearl, hasn't she always wanted one, a black pearl, or does she already have one, on her left middle finger, black against the white skin, from that big operation, such a large fee, what, yes, but will I be capable, will my hands be capable of cutting into someone's body now, a naked body, broken bones, straps and plaster and blood, chloroform and naked women...

'What's wrong with you, what's up, you've gone white all of a sudden,' his facial expressions are almost out of control and there's a hint of triumph in his voice, a glimmer of open hatred in his eye.

'Should I call your wife?'

Suddenly, the dog is standing in the room again; I hadn't noticed it sitting there the whole time, crouching under Borges's chair, its muzzle on its paws, but now it crawls out, stands up, slinks slowly out of the room, its tail tight between its legs.

'It's getting late,' I say at last while the other man, hunched in his silence, appears to have forgotten me. 'I'm sorry but I'll have to ask you to leave now. Grete has gone to lie down, the first day, getting used to everything again, takes a lot out of you, you know?'

'Oh yes, sorry,' the other man says, standing up. 'I didn't notice the time, I only meant to come for a moment to say hello to you and your wife and now, I'm sure, we're friends and will see quite a lot of each other.'

'Yes, we'll see quite a lot of each other.'

'And please apologize to Frau Grete for me too.'

He's gone: I walked him to the door and now I'm back in the room, I stand there alone for a moment, I need to hold on to the chair, overcome by a bout of light dizziness, everything's spinning around me, I can't think any more, I don't want to think any more, something inside me is hurting and will never be silent again, everything's so blurred, I don't know what I'm doing, there's a pain, a stabbing pain in my head, why did I let him in, why didn't I listen to Grete, he's stupid and harmless, maybe well-meaning too and only trying to scare me, it's dark now, enough now,

I want finally to get some rest and sleep, tomorrow's a new day, tomorrow...

Now she's in the room, 'Darling,' her voice says, caressing my neck tenderly, 'are you angry I went out, I couldn't stand him, I felt as if something was throttling me, and now you're not so jealous either, but I wanted to show you he means nothing to me...'

'Not to you and not to me either, everything's fine.'

Everything's fine for tonight, get some sleep first, tomorrow it begins, tomorrow...

'Did he say anything to you?'

'Inquisitive, are you—want to know every word, do you?'

'Hans!'

Dear me, how that exploded out of me, sharp as a whip-crack, I'd like to be so quiet with her, I'd like only ever to caress her; 'Hans,' her voice is like a barrel full of tenderness and humility, something melts in her eyes, her lips are moist, I bow over her face, which seems to be glowing from within, the lids close translucently over the twin blue stars, her long, dark lashes quiver, 'Come,' she whispers almost too quietly to hear, 'Mother dear is fast asleep, it must be late, that stupid man, I didn't look at the time, they're all asleep already, come, how I... long for you!'

I look at her, she's lying in my arms, her breath warm on my face, pure love radiating from her eyes. Suddenly, I am gripped by a terrible fear, my heart booming like a thunderstorm, something blocking my throat, what is all of this, when did I get here, it's night-time, this cannot go on, I want to be alone at last, I have to be alone, now, what does she want, why's she looking at me like this?!

She's sitting up, she hasn't noticed anything, her eyes are still on mine, they have to stay there for ever, they'll never leave, now she tucks her hand under my arm, with her left hand she opens the door, switches the light on inside, it's a small, yellow bulb, a gentle yellow glow, there are two beds, two beds side by side, no space between them, white sheets on both, a white eiderdown…

'No, no, no!'

Where did that scream come from, deep, unknown, horrible from inside my own body, she shrinks back in terror, eyes wide, trembling, pale to her fingertips, and looks at me.

'What's up with you, Hans?'

I too am shocked, I too am confused, I take her hands in mine, they're cold and clammy, I cover them with kisses, I wrap my arms around her waist, her body writhes with sobbing and shame, I pull her close to me, I sit down on the edge of the bed, pull her on to my lap, I see her white neck, her small, quivering tendons, her small, beating heart, my hand is over one of her rounded shoulders, her blouse snagged and tore on the bedpost as she moved, the white flesh shines dull and translucent, I press my lips to it, she forgets everything, blood is pounding in my temples, my hands wander wildly over her face, over the auburn hair, over the slender neck, the white breasts, the rounded knees… There's a scraping at the door, a scuffling and a scratching, I raise my head from the pillow, I listen out, my hands forget where they are, the fog is gone, everything is all sober and clear, all the attention is on the door; now come audible sounds of something skidding, wood splintering, I jump up, my shoes clatter and creak across the floorboards, I'm at the door, I fling it open, it's totally dark, there's no one there, maybe I was wrong, maybe it's just the hot blood in my ears or the shells from the battle, maybe I'm actually dead and dreaming the whole thing, someone's scratching on my coffin, the war's still going, bursting walls, mortar and mud, I try to shut the door again because it's absurd, standing by a door when there's no one there, I want to go back to her, how could I leave her on her own, but I have my hand on the door handle now, I'm pushing against it now and something soft and elastic is blocking it, suddenly I feel a terrible fear, I throw all my weight against it but the growling is getting louder and I can see two eyes very close to my face, big green eyes in the darkness, fixed, twinkling dots staring at me, and now a shaggy head too, bristling hair, a dark, shaggy body, braced as if to pounce, I take a blind step backwards, grab a chair from the corner, swing it into the air... the eyes have gone, the head's no longer there, the door yields and the latch clicks shut, I turn the key twice in the lock, whatever it is outside pads slowly away, and all is quiet again. I stand there for a moment longer, listening, there's not a sound, my breathing gradually slows to normal, I turn around, back towards the room, she's still lying there on the bed, she's turned onto her front, her head is buried, hot and red, in the pillows, her dress pulled up, her legs bare to above the knee, her hair in a loose coil, the bed shaking under her sobs. I go quietly over to her, suddenly she's a stranger to me, a total stranger, silently and carefully I pull the dress down over her legs, sit down on the edge of the bed, I'd like to say something to her, I'd like to reach out my hand and run my fingers through her hair, but it feels endlessly far, my hand is heavy and tired, my eyes are almost falling shut, I just want to sleep and sleep.

I don't know how long I've been sitting here, maybe I fell asleep, that's possible, I forgot I was sitting on a bed and have a weeping woman next to me, but I can't help it, I'm like Kaspar Hauser: coming out of a dark cellar, seeing light for the first time, a tree for the first time, a cloud, a stone, another person, a woman, my wife, memories come back very slowly, I need a lot of time, it's as if I'm sick, I'm seeing everything as if it's all new, I'm experiencing it all for the first time, it makes me so tired, the big, dark hand keeps coming back and covering everything over, I'm all alone again, it's so dreadful, the world and things and myself, most of all myself.

I shake myself awake, I can't just sit here, what time might it be, her slender hand resting on my hand, she's pulled the covers over her, the covers move very slowly, very evenly, it's her breathing, she's asleep.

Fraught, I study her features, she's lying on her back now, her face red and worn out from crying, one knee tucked up like a child, her eyelashes closed, messy little hairs curling out endearingly from her temples, her soft lips half open, now and again a deep sigh interrupts her easy breathing, then she squeezes my hand in her sleep, I don't move, I keep my head bowed over her, very close to her face, a small blue vein runs across the left side of her forehead and branches out over her temples; it's very quiet, just that regular breathing the whole time, always up and down, something's alive there, alive in its own right, constantly moving up and down, I can't stand it, I bend my head further over her, my lips touch hers, they're so soft, so sweet, I'm touching them, I'm touching life, now that life opens those lashes, dark-blue stars below me, emerging astonished from obscure, faraway dreams.

'Grete,' I say very quietly, 'I love you, I love your lips and the hairs on your forehead, I love your eyes and their distant shine, I love your tears and your weeping mouth, I was away for so long, but now I'm here, it'll take me some time to recognize you, be patient with me, I've a long way to go to find myself, things are hard for me, I have to look for myself first, but I love you, nothing can separate us now, I love you, always, from the core of my being, and I'll never let you go again.'

Two eyes wake up, two eyes listen, blue rays blaze from two eyes, two arms reach out and embrace my neck, a body rejoices, snuggles up tightly to mine, there are no clothes now, nothing more between us, lips on lips, body against body.

The night goes by, grey light creeps under the curtains, I can't sleep a wink, I push the covers off my chest, I lie there completely naked, I'm suffocating from the heat and strangeness. She's lying over in the other bed now, a smile flickers on her face, she's dreaming of me, even in her sleep I'm inside her, I'm not alone any more, why am I so restless, she will share everything with me, even if something should happen, but what can actually happen, Borges is my friend, he said so himself, he asked me to be friends, what can the dog do to me, and if it tries it again, I'll knock it to the floor, it's good that the night is over, anyone who tries to steal my good fortune, I'll knock them to the floor, they're no more than bad dreams and my head's aching, if only it wasn't so hot, the others are all asleep too, thick covers over their bodies, the boy and my mother, and only I'm awake because you have to keep watch, because something could happen any second, no one is safe from fate, you follow the threads, it's as if they run through the air, you feel your way along them and all of a sudden there are knots… 'Oh, you're awake, Grete, I thought you were asleep, why are you looking at me so strangely, why are you sitting up, what's wrong, I pushed the covers off because I was too hot, now I'm back under them, you're embarrassed, that's nice, but you see, in the war we forgot everything, even embarrassment, I don't sleep as well as you, so go on and speak, say something, your face has gone all white, everything's fine now though, I love you and you love me, we're starting a new life, we'll never be parted again, not even in our dreams, isn't that right, go on…'

'Pull... back... the covers... again,' she stammered breathlessly, 'I don't know, you look so strange, as if... You don't have a belly button!'

'No belly button? That's absurd, everyone has a belly button, everyone born to a mother, it's what links us to the earth, to all other people, we all have a mother, you're still sleeping, your eyes are all dreamy!'

'No, no, no,' she's in my bed with me, her small hand's suddenly full of force, she tears the covers off me, she stares at my body, there's horror in her eyes, now I look down too and touch my belly with my fingers: it's smooth, the skin taut as on a round drum, there's no dip there.

I don't have a belly button, I don't have a mother, I don't have a child, I'm not part of the chain that runs through all bodies from the first human to the last. I am not born of any womb, a body and yet not, me and yet someone else, a name, a fate and yet not a man. Where do I begin and where do I end? I can feel myself, I won't let all this be taken away from me.

'Grete? Don't be scared, it's smooth, the skin's all smooth, but maybe not totally smooth, look, here's a fold, a small one, but it's there, maybe something hit me there during the war, yes, a shell landed next to me, that must have been it, there was a huge explosion, I went flying, we were all sent flying to the ground, didn't I write to you about that?, the whole trench collapsed, we were all stunned, blood was pouring out of my body, I must have fallen on some barbed wire, not much, just a small wound, right here in the middle, look, and now there's a scar, now there's just this little line, a small fold, totally smooth, totally smooth already and nothing more to see, don't you believe that, don't you believe me?'

'You were wounded and you didn't write to tell me? Why didn't you write to tell me? I had a premonition, and my premonition was always that I could see you on the ground, buried under sand and earth, I always saw you bleeding and dead, Hans, oh Hans, you're here, it's over, you're alive, here, here's where it could have happened, here's where your lifeforce could have poured out, it would have been all over.'

She is beside herself, her lips and her hot cheeks are on my body, kissing the spot again and again, again and again. Then she sits up straight, kneels beside me, looks me straight in the eye.

'Why did you keep it from me? Because you love me, I know. But you don't know me, you don't know how brave I am and how strong, there's nothing you couldn't tell me, cannot tell me in the future. Whatever it might be, I'm not afraid.'

No. Nothing? Oh, to tell everything, to tell someone everything, to be able to let it all out like a storm! And what if I face her now, what if I stand up now, completely naked in this room, put her hand on the spot and tell her: Look, I don't have a belly button, no mother gave birth to me, none of this is true, I'm not human, I'm not me, I don't even know myself, but I love you… Then, then she will quake, then she will scream and push me away, oh, and then all that bravery and strength and all the love will be gone too?

'You're sad, my love, the past is all dead, we are here now and we are alive and we will be happy.'

We are here and we are alive. Yes, we will be happy. We have to be happy. We will have all the bravery and all the strength.

'It's already morning, it's already daytime, we should pull our clothes over our bodies.'

'What a strange thing to say: "pull our clothes over our bodies"!'

Strange? We slip into a costume, we drape a costume over our naked bodies, go to work and only then do we become people…

I have a white shirt against my skin, I'm wearing a light-grey suit, there's a fold in the light-grey trousers, my feet walk along in purple socks and brown shoes, I'm at work and they're sitting out there in the waiting room, I'm sitting in a comfortable chair at my desk, there's nothing remotely surprising about it, on the chair next to mine a woman is bowed over her child, it is six years old and cut its finger on a tin can while playing, I unwind the white bandage, the finger is red and swollen, a lifeless, doughy piece of flesh, like a separate body part, fine, red lines running up its arm, fine, pale-red ligaments, its narrow cheeks are flushed, its breath is racing, the round, brown eyes stare off into the distance with a feverish glint in them.

'Will you be able to save the finger, doctor? You said that if the fever hadn't come down by last night…'

A mother hangs on my words, my expressions, standing there, dissolving, wrestling but no tears are shed, her resolve is like a wall, letting nothing through, her tears trickling down inside her until it's full down there in that dark cavern, and her heart turns grey.

'What's his name?' I ask blankly in order to say something.

'Kurtchen, you know that…'

Oh yes, Kurtchen! A rounded, gentle name. But this finger, this fat, white bit of flesh—is that called Kurtchen too? Is it part of little Kurt? But Kurtchen battles it, battles himself, a bulwark against himself, all his blood corpuscles rush there, there's fighting in the tissue, Kurtchen is like a landscape, like a battlefield, there's a fight going on inside him, he isn't in his finger any more, he isn't his finger any more, the finger's all on its own, if we take it off with a knife and a saw, pull back the skin with forks, cut it out and sew the skin back over it, then what is that finger in the bucket, is that you too, Kurtchen, yesterday you were waggling it, grasping things and feeling them with it, yesterday it and four others reached for your mother's hand and it was happy—so where do you end, lying there in the bucket and sitting there in bed, you don't even need any fingers, we could cut off the whole arm, both arms and both legs, and where are you now, Kurtchen, where do you start and where do you end! You're not in any pain now, the nurse is bending over your head, pouring something onto the white fleece over your face, you breathe and can't feel anything any more, your heart's beating and cannot feel anything any more, you're alive and you don't know it, and I'm standing next to you and am not alive and yet I think I am, I'm standing here in my white coat, blood flowing through me and around me, spraying onto white sheets and gauze, people's blood, there's part of their life on that gauze, I have silver instruments and use them to clamp off life, lying in the bucket are splinters of bone and bits of stomach and gut and limbs, and in the beds lie the people they belonged to, and I walk through all of this, breathing, there's breathing inside me, I ask about fever and pain, I palpate bodies and bend over torsos, my ear is above their lung and their heart, it's beating all by itself, and they don't feel it, can't feel themselves, I hear the breathing and the beating, I can look inside them, I know the rhythms of their lives, I see the small bacteria at work, I sit at my microscope and stare at a blot, I turn knobs and see fine patterns and stitches, cells in the tissues, blue and red dots and rods, bacteria that got there from outside, and the blood corpuscles they're driving out. But they lie asleep in bed next door and have no idea that I can see things about them that they never knew and never will.

Oh, all life is blind, I know everything, I see everything, I help everyone, apart from myself, our eyes always look outwards, but inside there is a dark cavern and we're inside it and can never see ourselves.

Grete? Yes, that's enough for today, but maybe someone will die tonight, the beating in their chest will stop and at that moment I'm lying alongside you, embracing you, and my life and my seed flow into you, happiness unites us, and while one new life begins here, another is snuffed out there and goes somewhere no one can follow it.

'You look tired,' she says. 'I haven't seen those lines around your mouth before, you should have rested for a few days first and not started working full time, it's getting to you more than usual, it's as if they've all been waiting for you to get back, there are other doctors out there…'

'And you?'

'I'm happy, and I think of nothing but you.'

'And Borges?'

'Is far away.'

'But what if he comes now?'

'He won't come, and even if he did… Why torment us both? You know I don't love him.'

'And the whole time I was out there, lying in a trench, there was no one with you, always alone, with no man desiring you?'

She bursts into tears.

'Ah, you women always cry when you can't see any other way out!'

'You've been working too hard, you're just wound up again—'

'Because I've guessed the truth—'

'You know it isn't the truth.'

'You—'

'Don't hit me, you know what's it's like.'

She's trembling, she has bowed her head, what am I doing, why does it keep spilling out of me, why am I like this, and why am I working so hard, what do I care about the sick! Not to work for once, celebrate life, that's what we're made for, that's… what we've made ourselves into!

'Frau Bussy Sandor—'

'Quick, wipe away those tears!'

'Now, if I happened to be jealous too…' she says with a quiet smile and dabs her eyes with the white cloth.

There's an unease in me, a strange tension I don't understand, I've gone over to the door, I've almost forgotten Grete, my steps are light and bouncy, I feel young and elegant, but at the same time my heart is beating anxiously, with a twinge in my chest like a knife wound when this woman comes waltzing in with small, rapid steps, her smooth, black hair swept back severely from her white forehead, black lashes, straight, black eyebrows, complexion as translucent as white marble, and those big eyes, opaque and boring into me; I know this look, it both commands and pleads, seduces and dictates, and yet it seems so meek. But when those lashes sink and the gaze becomes hooded, a moist gleam coats the darkness, the white takes on a bluish shimmer, the round, black pupils dart under the cover of the lids, and the slim mouth opens purply soft, as the neck tilts submissively to one side.

But now there's a smile around this mouth, which is hard and narrow and closed, it forcibly composes itself, there's a flicker in her eyes, the left hand clutches a tissue tightly and crumples it frenziedly between white fingers. She walks over to Grete, she embraces her and as the two women's cheeks touch for a second, she looks over her shoulder, past her, staring straight at me, gloating with a triumphant yet pleading smile.

This woman is horrible, the thought strikes me; I would really rather be outside right now, never meet her again, who knows why, and a dull fear suddenly brushes me: she needs to let go of Grete, I can't leave the two of them together like this, then suddenly the dog's in the room again too, I almost love it now, it isn't looking at me but staring slobbering at them, it keeps appearing, like a ghost, it's limping, its left paw dragging along behind, pulled up and shorter than the right leg, it's sticky with blood, but I can't see any fresh blood now, it's from during the night, I almost pity it, why does it stand there like a ghost in the doorway, it can be glad that I didn't shoot it, why does it keep sniffing, that perfume, it's like her, heavy and intoxicating, there's something cruel about it, it gets into your brain, the blood begins to circulate, a red mist… it can make you forget things, you have to sink right into it, experience things you've never experienced before: crime… murder… desire…

She holds out her hand for me to kiss, I bow over it, a dark wave surges into my temples, it feels as if someone's poured lead over my brain, I bend my neck and feel a nameless hatred, but when my face re-emerges, it wears a smile like hers.

'You were gone a long time, my friend, and time dragged for all of us,' her voice is deep and soft as a bed, as if her lips are savouring every word before speaking it.

'I was busy, the war…'

'Yes, you were such a hero, always at the very front, operating in the hail of bullets, no qualms, duty comes before all else, doesn't it, and death we can die many times…'

'He was wounded…'

'Wounded?' She grabs my arm, her scorn is all gone, all the masks are gone, all precaution dropped, and in two strides she is with me, and on her face is written only fear, only passion, only love. For no more than a second, then she has mastered herself again, on her lips again the lovable, scornful smile, no more than a quiet quaver in her voice now, she turns to Grete, she threads her arm through hers.

'See, my love, that's how men can be. Ruthless and selfish. But now you have him back.'

For a second she glares at me, a spark of open contempt in her eye, it sounds like a challenge, and in that second I hate her; I think of Borges, I don't know why, what do all these people want from me, crowding in on me, stalking me, snatching at me with their arms, I want some peace, I just want a little happiness, they should all leave, I want to be alone with Grete, I don't know anyone, I want to be alone!

'You went straight back to work, of course, you've got a lot to do, I can imagine, and he has to go out in the evening and at night, and you sit at home all alone and wait for him, but you can be sure that he doesn't do so willingly, he'll devote all the time he has to you, that's how it always was and that's how it's going to be from now on.'

'Where would I be otherwise, isn't it obvious?'

There's a nasty curl to her lips now, she comes very close to me, her perfume, the scent coming off her skin is intoxicating, her left eyebrow twitches nervously.

'Don't be scared. Was it so easy to lose your friends?'

What does she want, what's she threatening?

'That's exactly why our friends think highly of us,' Grete says. 'Do you think my husband would have that large practice if he didn't give his all for his patients? He does his duty and I do mine by staying in the background and helping him, I love him for his sense of duty, his profession brings responsibility, so everything has to be quiet all around, I couldn't imagine it any other way, it's normal.'

My heart is pounding, what am I scared of, Grete is right, of course, the child with the finger, the others too, all normal, but I'm uncertain now, I feel tense inside, my brain is tired and feels battered, I can barely stand upright, I don't feel well:

'Maybe we should go and eat together somewhere, it was a bit much today after all, it takes getting used to, maybe to a restaurant or—'

'You look terrible, did something go wrong?'

'No, no.'

'Come to the theatre or the opera! Light, music, people, there's room for us all in my box.'

Is she winking at me?

'Those stupid actors in their phony spotlights! Prancing around in their made-up roles for an evening, where they have their destinies and feel important and put on airs, and yet back home they're poor wretches, surviving on the bare minimum and dulled emotions like pastry chefs.'

'Let's stay at home,' I say, 'everything's fine.'

'What's wrong with you—something spoil your mood? If you want to go, I'll come with you, Frau Bussy's offer—'

'Maybe he's scared of seeing so many people. Another suggestion: let's go to the observatory and look at the stars. It's empty there—and dark,' she adds in a whisper, the back of her hand seeming to touch mine accidentally, like a caress, or am I imagining things—did I want to do it, was it me who did it? I look timidly at her face, it is cold and blank.

'A delightful idea,' Grete says happily, 'something completely new, let me give you a hug, I've always wanted to see it, you too, haven't you… or shouldn't we even ask you?'

She's suddenly all bright and young like a child, she walks out of the room, head held high, her whole figure, her hair, like a dance, how I love her now, that there is a woman like her!

Someone grabs my arm from behind, hot and hard, it's like the slender talon of a bird of prey, and Bussy's face is close to mine, her cheeks glowing, her eyes twinkling with restrained fire.

'Why didn't you answer my letters,' she spits in a rush, 'and why all this stupid act of going away! What do we need her for! I want you to myself, all to myself! Come tomorrow, tomorrow afternoon, you…'

Her arms are on my chest, wrapping themselves around my neck, her lips, I'm going nuts, 'Don't you love me any more?' she hisses. 'Rue coming back, do you? To that woman?'

Why don't I tear myself free from these arms? Why don't I shove her away from me? Why am I on fire at this kiss, when this woman, when Grete is…

She's let go of me, I'm standing here on my own again, Grete has her hat and her black coat, still smiling, a little dimple on the left cheek there, I force my panting breath back down into my chest, I'm totally numb…

'Why are you smiling?' Grete asks me brightly. 'You're both making faces as if you were planning a surprise.'

A surprise, yes, that's funny, we mustn't give anything away, what do I mean, has she told her, I can't think straight, the perfume is on my jacket now, I'll smell it tomorrow while I'm working, but it's horrible, maybe I'm actually anaesthetized, someone else is the doctor and I'm undergoing all of this, none of it affects me while I try simply to swim on top of the wave, on the ocean, free as can be, free as can be…

'That coat really suits you,' Bussy says now, and her arm is around Grete's neck, her voice almost cowering, arching her back; she's like a black cat.

Borges is standing down in the street, where did he come from, has he been standing there the whole time, he doesn't appear to have been expecting us, his face is tilted up towards the window, all feverish, he's white as a ghost, his head buried between hunched shoulders, his lips all tight and clenched, his entire body crumpled. Now he's spotted us, he gives a start, his shoulders twitch as if in spasm, he draws himself up, with a timid, almost childish smile on his face, he bows to Grete, he kisses her hand stiffly and greets us too.

'Where did you appear from,' Bussy grunts at him, 'you look like a lunatic!'

'I, um… evening, um… I just wanted… the air is refreshing now.'

'Well, join us,' and she shoots me a sly look, 'there are three of us, and four's better for walking. We're marching to the stars.'

'If I may…'

Bussy presses up against me, I see through this ruse, she wants him for Grete, she wants to split me off from her, she wants to be next to me, she wants to hold my hand in the dark, she wants to tilt her head a bit to the left, I'll look into her eyes, her hair will brush my cheek… I don't want that!!

'Madam,' Borges says, offering her his arm, which she has no choice but to take, she's furious.

Borges? What's Borges after with Bussy? A trap? What's Bussy to him? And Grete? She's left standing on her own, she gives me a helpless, beseeching look, I'm there with her, I forget everything, I grab her arm, we walk off without looking back.

'See,' she says happily, 'he had no interest in walking with me, he's avoiding it, it's almost as if he's scared of me.'

'He loves you,' I say and press her arm tightly against mine, 'he's walking along behind us with Bussy to ogle your legs. Can't you feel his eyes on your back?'

'Why would I care?'

I'm very happy as we go through the dark streets and she hangs on my arm, people come past us, some of them greeting us and oddly delighted to see me, but they must know me or maybe they think I'm someone else, what does it matter.

'See, no one's forgotten you,' Grete says.

No, I don't forget either... something that is inside you once must stay there somewhere, and it makes no difference... so they know me, there's nothing special about that, it is so nice to walk like this, it is all the same if the other two are behind us, the two of them are like dogs, it's very droll, but Nero's there now, Nero in the flesh, how did that dog get here? 'Didn't you lock him in the flat, Grete?'

'Maybe Mother let him out, it doesn't matter.'

Mother? No, it doesn't matter, everything else is irrelevant now, we walk briskly so that the others can't catch up with us, the dog bouncing and barking around us, and he seems happy too; we've reached the station, we buy tickets and are already at the top of the steps, the right train is just leaving, we're in the compartment, we're moving, the dog is with us, Borges and that Sandor woman will have to wait for ten minutes, hurray! the man on the opposite bench stares at us so strangely, yes, we're lovers and if I want, I can take Grete and kiss her, if I want, and he can pull that face if he likes; I take Grete's hand and whisper this in her ear, she blushes, she's so beautiful when she blushes, she laughs at me brightly with her happy eyes, the dog has rested its muzzle on her lap and shut its eyes, she has one arm in mine, the other hand is stroking the dog's fur, not that I mind, it's a pathetic creature, I want to stroke it too but it immediately starts growling, so stupidly, and now it moves away from Grete too, shakes itself, lies down on its own in the dusty corner under the bench with its head on its paws, and looks at me with such sadness in its eyes as if it's crying, *can* dogs cry?

    The train stops, we've arrived, but we're going to have to wait for the others, Bussy will be angry, might she be giving Borges the same sideways look, not that Borges will care, nor can I get rid of her perfume, and I'll have to put on a different coat tomorrow. We won't wait, will we, Grete; they'll know the way without us and of course they can ask, Borges is good at reconnaissance, ha-ha, not many streetlights here, it's properly dark, Nero has his nose to the ground and trots silently along behind us with his tail hanging low, how quiet it is among those trees, it's pretty late, what is time, there's no such thing as time, our footsteps are completely regular, it's as if they're alone in this silence, just our feet walking alongside each other now, my big shoes and her small ones, and it's the two of us, the echoes, the two of us alone in the middle of all this space, on and on, it seems normal now, the feet move of their own accord, just as the heart beats of its own accord until it stops, of its own accord; footsteps come towards us now on the other side, advancing very slowly and calmly, this is a person who is calm, a heart that is calm, we should be like that too, now he's level with us, he's smoking a cigar, we can see a red glow, everything else is one big black shadow, doesn't he have anyone walking alongside him like me, I have someone, yes, the most beautiful woman, and she loves me and we are happy, now the steps die away, leaving only ours.

Now we're there, above us the dome of the observatory is half open, turning noiselessly on its rails, the tube pointing up weirdly into the night like a giant cannon, and star twinkles alongside star in the cloudless sky. We go inside, an old man comes towards us, he has white hair and a white beard, his eyes are ice-grey, he speaks in a quiet whisper, our feet ring out hard on the cement, we tell the old man we want to wait for a little, but he doesn't seem to hear us, he's deaf, he must have been listening hard up here for so long that he can't hear anything now, he goes up his steps without a thought for us, sits down at the instrument and begins twiddling the knobs, his hand dwarf-like and dark brown, blue veins streaking through it as if through old wood, sitting there all scrunched up on his chair with his spindly, protruding neck like some ancient bird, his eyes already millions of miles away, only his body left sitting there, glued small and fragile to the end of the telescope, seemingly lifeless, rattled by the occasional cough, then tensing up, turning blue and jerking this way and that, but head and eye stay calm and stuck to the tube, he doesn't flinch, he notices none of this, he's out there, far away out there. Now he starts to mumble, it's hard to understand, he only has a few brown teeth left, why bother about your teeth, and I focus closely on his lips, which say, 'Light years... planetary orbits... helium gas', it's as if they're feeling these words that seem like drops spinning off whatever is vibrating out there.

'He looks like a billy goat,' Bussy says, giggling and pointing at the old man with her eyes.

I didn't even notice her arrive, how long have we been here, she seems cross with me and doesn't look at me, agitated, her nostrils flaring open and closed, she blunders loudly from one object to the next, commenting on everything, touching everything, twisting every knob. Borges clings to her side, he seems to have forgotten all about Grete and lets out loud, unrestrained guffaws at Bussy's stupid remarks. Finally they stop.

'So, where are the stars... they're just stupid machines no one understands!'

She's standing next to the man up there at the eyepiece, the little body there oblivious to her, both her eyes and her soft limbs and her perfume; there's a silence in the room that affects even her, no one dares breathe, there's a sense of something holy in this musty air, and for a moment she hesitates, staring at the old, frail man, before tapping sheepishly on the bent back and saying somewhat uncertainly, 'Hey, Herr Professor, you've been looking at all that for a hundred years or more, give someone else a go for once!'

Slowly the old man peels himself from his instrument and gives her a perplexed look, his eyes still far out in those expanses of fog-shrouded stars and boundless space.

'Yes, yes,' he says, nodding his old head mechanically. 'Yes, yes, three trillion… three, I tell you!'

One after another we go up the steps, my heart's pounding, Bussy's already sitting on the chair, crosses her legs so that her skirt rides up to her knee, her cheerfulness unassailable, and she calls Saturn a cartwheel and says Sirius would make a good tiepin, her mouth moving incessantly, she wants to see every star, but at last she's had enough, slides off her chair, offering a glimpse of her green garter, makes way with a graceful movement for Borges, who's seen it all before, isn't interested, leaves it to the scientists, and finally Grete is up there, a little clumsy, confused, can't get her bearings at first, can't see anything, but then her face begins to glow, 'How beautiful,' she says simply and sincerely, looking like a silent Madonna, with something like piety on her face, then she gets up, grasps my coat in her left hand and says, 'Have a look, Hans, you have to see this!' All right, so now I go up to it, but just as I'm sitting down and bringing my head to the instrument and looking out into the infinite space, a voice reaches me from out there, from the wide, empty universe, a solitary, whining soul complaining and calling me and finding no peace. Dread grips me, it's horrible, coming in from out there in the cold, my heart clenches, a chill freezes my veins, maybe I can only hear it inside me, but now it's a clear and heart-wrenching weeping, like a child or a dead person weeping, myself weeping, the air in front of my eyes starts to flicker, I see green and red circles, a large green and gold disc quivers in the lens, is it in my brain or a distant sun, Sirius, I think, there may be living beings there, a bit of me is far out there, a part of me, I can see it there now, back when the ancient Egyptians were still around, I wasn't even born, I can see the past, I can see it with my own eyes, the light has taken so long to get here, maybe it's actually already gone out, no one knows, I'm a ray of light too, maybe I'm already dead out there and calling out to myself through cold space and hearing myself and seeing myself and maybe I'm not even here…

That whining, that horrible whining… now it's gone quiet.

'Thank God,' Grete's voice says beside me at the same moment, 'the stupid creature has finally stopped, but that'll be the last time it comes with us.'

'Who? The dog?' I say, and my teeth are chattering as if I've got a fever.

'Didn't you hear it? The moment you sat down at the instrument... who was looking after it before, it was lying there completely calm in the corner; it jumped up, sniffed around the instrument and started whimpering and howling so pathetically...'

'I heard it too, yes, I heard it too,' I say through pallid lips, 'maybe it smelt something, something or other, just leave it, and we'll go home now.'

We go back the same way in silence, Bussy and Borges chatting away a little ahead of us, but Grete is silent too, she can sense my suffering, occasionally she gives me a worried sideways look I'm not meant to notice, then squeezes my arm tighter, she doesn't ask anything and I'm grateful for that. The dog walks in front of us, always to Borges and Bussy and then back, probably a hundred times, its tongue hanging out until finally we've reached our front door and say goodbye.

'Tomorrow at four,' Bussy whispers to me, looking at me just once, an abyss flaring in her eyes. I quickly forget her and go to my room.

'Don't you want to go to bed, it's very late,' Grete says.

'Very late, yes,' I repeat absentmindedly. 'I want to go in and see the kid again!'

'Now, in the middle of the night?'

I'm already at his bedside, I pick up the little sleeper, take his little hands in mine, stroke those little feet, I kiss him quietly on the eyes, lay him back down in the cradle, carefully pull up the blanket, turn round, try to say something... and suddenly I throw myself down at Grete's feet in shocked disbelief.

'For heaven's sake, what's got into you, my darling,' she cries breathlessly and tries to pull me up, but I fling my arms around her dear body, hug her knees, bury my head in the folds of her dress and sob, 'A child like that; a child like that, yours and mine… never, never!'

She pulls me up, takes me on her lap like a child, runs her fingers quietly over my hair, her bewildered eyes peering large and deadly serious and questioning into mine, her lips move, but not a word comes out. We slept no more that night…

I dream that I'm sitting curled up in a round tube so no one can see me, it's a telescope and I'm holding it the wrong way round, and I see myself at the other end, small and far away, I turn the knob and the face gets closer and sharper, but it isn't me, it's someone else, so I turn it this way and that, and the face keeps changing. Then Grete is inside it, but she also grows further and further away. Suddenly Borges is sitting next to me in the tube, we're throwing dice for Grete and Bussy, he bets his tiepin, which is Saturn, and I bet my head, which is Sirius. Then the tube fires, I always suspected it was actually a cannon and that it would have to fire one day, it must have been Borges who put in the gunpowder, I'm gripped by an unspeakable anger, we're tumbling through space, with him always a few light years ahead of me and so are Grete and Bussy, each of them very distant and round and gleaming, and in the middle is a sun, that's me, I stretch my hands out longingly towards it and still can't touch myself. Eventually, at the very end, there's the dog, it opens its jaws very wide, I grab Sirius and try to hurl it at the dog and hit Borges who tumbles and now we all fly into the jaws, Bussy and Borges and Grete, Sirius and Saturn and me, and it gets very dark and tears trickle from the animal's eyes like drops of gold onto the round, black earth…

I wake up, I look at Grete lying there next to me with her motionless blue eye-stars on the ceiling, her face wet with tears, I kiss her very quietly on the forehead, she throws both arms around me, full of such passion that I almost dissolve.

'Hans, Hansi!' she says into my hot ear. 'Now you don't believe this either, you don't even believe it's our child, what am I supposed to do, you have a kind of sickness inside, why are you torturing me like this, you were always jealous but now you're suspicious about the child… I've been wondering all night how to prove my love for you, but how can I if you don't believe me, if… I can't go on like this.'

Her voice is choked with sobs.

'It isn't that, you don't understand,' I say, rattled, 'I can't tell you.'

'What is it you can't tell me, you're hiding something from me, I know, but if you love another woman more than me, then tell me, speak to me, even if it breaks me… I'll do anything for you, I'll put up with anything, I only want you to be happy because I love you so, love you so much.'

Oh, I feel so sick, I can't stand this torment, if only I could speak, if only I were dead.

'No, I love no one but you, you needn't think about anything nor have any doubts, everything's all right, definitely, it'll all come good, just have patience with me, just have a little patience!'

I go out, what else can I do, there's no point in anything. Outside is Mother.

'Where is Grete?' she asks, glancing sideways at me, her thin, crinkled lips resting on top of each other, quivering impotently this way and that.

'In bed. She'll be out in a little while, she doesn't feel very well.'

'Then sit down here for a while next to your old mother if it doesn't bore you. And push the chair in for me so we can have breakfast together, I can't really be alone.'

'Yes… Mother.'

I move her chair closer and sit down at the table as well, I push the cup towards her and pour her some coffee, I don't know what to say, I start eating and she takes one of the buns too, breaks it apart with spindly fingers, her glasses peer down diagonally at the cup, piece by piece she crumbles the hunk of bread into the bitter beverage, then takes three lumps of sugar, it must taste disgustingly sweet, I think, and how unattractive those fingers are, how chewed the nails and then: she's my mother, I have to talk to her, but what can I say to her?

'This bread is so hard, my teeth can't bite through it,' she mumbles to herself. 'The baker's no good any more, used to be a lot better, we'll have to go to a different one.'

'Yes,' I say, seizing on this, 'I will, it was only in the oven for half an hour too long, they didn't knead it enough either, look, this bit here, leave it to me, I'll go and see them in a minute, the apprentice wasn't paying attention, that's all.'

'What do you know about these things? You're talking as if you've done nothing but bake buns your whole life.'

She's shaking with laughter, but a crumb must have got stuck in her throat because she starts coughing, a nasty, hard cough, she turns blue all over and writhes over her plate, I jump up in shock, feeling very strange, I've gone red up to my forehead, bread like this, a crumb like that can kill you, what do I care about the buns, where would I, a doctor, have learnt about them, it would be important for people with stomach trouble, all of us doctors should learn to cook, invent new recipes, maybe we could extend the laboratory, knowledge is always good, the consistency of pasta, how the gastric glands react to different types of flour…

She's calmed down now, she's sitting there again with her coffee, mumbling incomprehensibly to herself, what do I care, I'm out of time, I have to work, do my duty, 'that's why I love him,' Grete says… Work and work, what else is there?

There's some post lying on my desk, letters from other doctors, letters from patients wanting my advice, from friends, from scientific societies, from the court, what business do

I have with the court, it's a large, grey envelope, there's a small parcel inside it, a small wooden box, I open it first, there's a little tube inside, bedded on cotton wool, I break the seal, there's cartilage and skin, human skin it must be, an Adam's apple, dents in the skin, a bite, a wound. I tear the letter open, they're asking me to examine it, write a report for the court, a murder, a maid bit through her employer's Adam's apple, in bed—the things that happen—because he was raping her, she'd wanted money for her mother in distress, the employer had promised her beforehand and then refused when he'd got what he wanted, so she bit though his Adam's apple. Or was it a dog, a dog was apparently there too, no one recognized it, the woman from the boarding house let him bound into the room at the exact time of the crime, maybe the girl is innocent, maybe it was a dog bite and the blood is the dog's blood, not human blood, that can be established, of course, they could also have sent me the specimen a bit earlier, the trial's at twelve and now the operation, the appendix one, at four I'm meant to meet Bussy, oh Bussy, that crazy woman, she torments you mercilessly, over and over again, I shouldn't really go, it's Borges who signed the document, he's the lead prosecutor of course, a vile job, but if it's murder then the examination will be quick, microscope, a quick smear on the slide, the blood cells are dyed, the white ones with the blue nuclei, the red ones... Of course they're from a human, it must have been murder, it is murder, and now it's time to operate!

He's already strapped to the white table, wrists attached, a broad belt across his legs, he's already asleep, the body rears up one last time, the muscles go into spasm, the face behind the white mask is red and swollen, the nurse pulls up his left eyelid and probes his eye with her fingertip, he is only twitching a little now, is this still a human being, his whole body slackens, the breathing gets deeper, the lungs blow the air out and in, he's sleeping, where is he now, he isn't aware of being alive now, we could leave him to sleep for ever, until he's dead, why does this occur to me now; I hate these appendix operations, maybe he'll recover without an operation, it's often turned out like that, we shouldn't operate on anyone at all, everyone should die when they die, no sticking the knife in, slicing through the skin into the middle of the body. I've finished washing now, my hands are clean, no more bacteria on them, we always carry billions of them on us, we have enemies like these everywhere without knowing it, and they're alive too, they have rights too, no more and no fewer than we do, we should stop doing anything, no one's guilty, anywhere we lay our hand and make a movement, right away there's guilt, immediately there's injustice and death, Borges doesn't understand that, he's incapable of understanding it, a man like him will never grasp that, there's only ever guilt or non-guilt, someone is dead, so someone must be guilty, but there are things... what do I care about him!

I have rubber boots on my feet, a rubber apron around my waist, a sterile white coat on top, I pick up the coat with splayed red fingers so I don't have to touch it, I have thin sterile gloves and a sterile, round, white cap on my head, the ether fills my eyes with sweet, acrid steam, I look like a baker, everyone's a baker in these caps, the cake's done now, and we cut into it as a test, an air bubble bursts, no, it's a blood vessel, it sprays a little red fountain of blood, there are lots and lots of little red dots on the white sheet, like little red strawberries on a white cream tart, that's a ridiculous comparison, we have to clamp it or it'll keep on bleeding and his life will seep away, and another one dies, dead from appendicitis, go on, just pull back the muscles with the fork, there needs to be room, there's the peritoneum, it's very thin and keeps moving this way and that, so there's some sensation after all, still here, one bit is more sensitive than another, you have to open up the stomach to find out, he needs more anaesthetic, he's remembered he's alive and that he's a person lying here, the body tries to jerk upwards, but he's already asleep again, and there's the intestine, there's a bit of murky fluid there, the appendix, the little vermiform appendage has to be taken off with a hot cauter inside the living body, it's out now, it's red and inflamed with a small, grey swelling on the wall, let him wake up, do the last few stitches yourself, so you have a thing like that in your body and it's completely unnecessary, it serves no purpose now, just a left-over from our animal ancestor, senselessly passed down and inherited through the chain, our parents aren't our father and mother, not their blood alone, we have every animal inside us, every plant, all of them speaking their parts inside us, speaking their muffled language, as embryos we still have all their shapes, breathing with gills, we're fish and reptiles and animals, the whole of creation is inside us, then we do something and move around, but we're merely the final product, the sum of everything, where do we stop, we're all brothers, we're all one, there's no guilt because we're not ourselves, that's our eternity, there's none other than this, we don't need heaven, we're always here, we were always here, we're in all people and all things and the whole world.

It's already half past eleven, we need to get dressed, I'd like to go and see Grete again but it's too late now, I have to put on a black coat, the court is harsh, everything is dark and cruel, they stand there and condemn unknown people and unknown lives, what drove such a poor girl to murder, it's understandable, this rich gentleman's probably a villain, the man is always guilty and the woman pays, and the girl did it for her mother in distress, she'll have taken some pleasure from it, of course, there's a charity for every kind of misery, there was a brother too, a blacksmith or a baker, definitely not a baker, he was killed in action, might have been able to help by working, there would have been no misery, a person would still be alive, a woman guilt-free. What might she look like: probably one of those black, blood-thirsty imps with plump red lips and a good deal of cheek, he won't have been the first she offered herself to either, the whole thing's probably just a sentimental comedy to win some sympathy, contrived to put the court in a more lenient state of mind, innocence and poor mother and misery, with the bread-winning brother killed in action. She's just a whore he didn't pay enough, then they have an argument and she crushes his throat. But so what, I must do my duty, make a statement, it's human blood, your honours, and that's all there is to say.

It's raining, the light from the sky is wan, the car bounces through the Tiergarten, across the Grosser Stern roundabout and to the bridge, there's a girl standing on the corner, she's blonde and wearing a white blouse, she smiles at me, just some stranger inside the car, and she blushes, she's waiting to cross the embankment, the car whips through a puddle and yellow mud sprays her fine stockings, and something boils up inside me, I want to ask the driver to slow down, my voice trembles, a strange restlessness inside me, why am I so worked up, I twist round to wave an apology and all I can see is the face looking down and hands grabbing the white dress and yanking it up.

The car stops outside the criminal court, I'm feeling tetchy and on edge, I get out, I wander along corridors and up steps, a few people are standing around, dark clusters too, no one dares to speak loudly, it's the house of destiny, I show a court clerk my summons and he points me with a yawn towards a side corridor, I read the numbers above the room doors, I'm very tired, hoping it won't go on for long, I can make my statement and be back home again—home, yes, a strange and beautiful word, does anybody have a home?

I'm sitting in my seat, the public are tightly packed on the benches—what are they all doing here, pure curiosity... Borges is already standing at his lectern, his face bright red, he doesn't see me, he's absorbed in reading the files, I'm here far too early, I'd have been better off coming on foot than spraying strangers with that car, or I should have gone to see Grete after all, it seems as if the whole thing holds some great importance for me and all because of some nasty, bestial crime, I'm a doctor, not a lawyer, the barrister over there with his pince-nez doesn't look particularly intelligent, if he's got time to talk to other people and crack jokes then he isn't taking the matter very seriously; he's used to this but is that allowed if you're meant to be rescuing a person from death or from prison, a girl like this... the judges are on their way, they're taking their seats at last, always the same ritual crap, the defendant... I can't see properly, this rainy weather, it's half-dark up there, they really didn't need to have two police officers escort her, the public crane their necks as if they're at the circus, a human being is a human being, and if she has done it, committed a crime, then she still resembles a human being, no different from anyone else, but now she's speaking: Name? 'Emma Bettuch', she's blonde, of course, Emma Bettuch, Bettuch, Bettuch?! The public laugh out loud, of course, they shouldn't laugh, it's a respectable name, there's nothing funny about it, the same old laughter, that same giggling, someone should give these oafs a good beating! Emma? They probably call her Emmy.

Emmy? I need to see her, what does her voice sound like, who is this Bettuch?

I stand up, someone behind me shouts 'Sit down!', of course, this isn't the circus, I'm going to be waiting a while to give my statement, Mother may still be sitting there with her cup of coffee, Mother? It's going to be a long journey, Grete can't come along either, it's sad how soft the girl's voice is, and how sad, she's no criminal, no way, just a poor wretch, a sick wretch who ought to be in my care, I should get up and take her with me, I'm entitled to do that, I'm the only one who realizes, I'm a doctor, they should all leave her alone, we are all brothers and sisters we are all equally guilty and equally innocent, I want to go to her, she's still a child, what have they done to her!

Now she's speaking, very quietly, as if she was standing on tiptoe and whispering something very tenderly into my ear, Father died very early on, oh no, and Mother's sick, Mother's sick?! Very sick, she doesn't say what's wrong with her, she keeps talking about her brother who was a baker and fed the family and went to the front and died on the very last day, they'd got everything ready for his return, they'd baked a big cake, the young, former apprentice made it with barley flour and raisins, the cack-handed rascal, no way it could ever have turned out right, Mother had them move her chair over to the window and was always on the lookout, they've got everything clean and gleaming and spread out fir branches and woven a big wreath, the bed upstairs is freshly made for him, she had to buy new white sheets as a surprise for him, Mother has handed over the last of her savings, but when the brother gets here there'll be money coming into the house again, he'll take over the bakery again straight away, people always need bread rolls, everyone has to eat, a guaranteed source of income and they only come home once, so many of his comrades killed, so many desperate families, and they alone get to welcome home their hero, their saviour.

Darkness fell and still he hadn't come, maybe he hadn't caught the regular train, they were all so packed, nothing worked any more, the revolution came so suddenly, then all bonds were broken, all peace and quiet gone, everyone wanted to get home, so you had no choice but to wait. 'Keep to the point, please,' the judge says, but isn't this the point, isn't this... For a moment she's confused, her voice becomes even smaller and more timid, fluttering around like a poor, lost bird, what more does she have to tell, after all this is the most important thing, he didn't come, they sat there for four more days, the flowers were completely wilted, Mother completely frozen, she couldn't believe it, her face turned grey but no tears ran down her cheeks, everyone came home, but not Wilhelm, not Wilhelm... Wilhelm Bettuch was missing, no one had seen him killed, comrades came home and they knew nothing, Emmy spent hours queuing in government offices, they knew nothing, Mother moved her chair away from the window again, she shed no tears, but Emmy heard moans in the night, as if from a 'broken jug', where did she get that expression—her brother had always said it! Now Mother can hardly get out of bed any more, her heart is failing, things have got much worse lately because of all the agitation and the silent despair, Emmy has to work, get a job, earn some money, did she ever have to do that before, Mother makes a fuss, but it's no use, are they to starve, she has to, but she knows no trade, she's been at home the whole time, helping Mother and making herself pretty for the brother, who loved her more tenderly than anyone, she still has his picture, it's still there on her bedside table, now she puts it inside her blouse, like the portrait of a lover, does she smile? and kisses the mother goodbye, she's choking, she doesn't have any medicine left, there's not a penny in the house, someone has to earn some money and now it's down to her, she looks around for a long time, all the jobs are taken by men returning from the battlefield, there's nothing, finally she goes to Berlin, she reads a small ad for a maid on a country estate near Friedrichshagen, a maid's job, but there's no choice, those delicate hands are going to be raw and red, there's no choice, they'll order her around, maybe hit her, doesn't matter, just money, money, they need a doctor when the mother dies, it doesn't bear thinking about, that's expensive, medicine, fine food, oh, she'll do anything, she's already out there, the landowner gives her a look that makes her want to punch him in the face… Money: he's short and has fat arms, fat, fleshy hands, reddish hair and a brutal mouth, he has a squint and he looks her up and down… Just money: the wife immediately barks at her, she's old and skinny and has a pair of cut diamonds in her ears, laughs at Emmy's dress, now she has to wear a coarse apron, good thing her brother can't see her, she has to help the groom to shovel the manure out of the stables, that's not in her contract, she's angry, complains to the husband, the woman nearly slaps her, she takes it quietly, money, money, money, the husband, the landowner, looks at her ever more strangely, in the garden one day at noon—the wife has gone out—he grabs her around the waist, she squirms out of his grasp, now her life becomes hell, the wife finds out, becomes suspicious, gets jealous and it's hell now, she starts to hate her, it gets worse and worse, one evening the husband goes off to Berlin, tells her to come with him, pack quickly, she, the maid, is to go with him, maybe he'll buy something and she'll have to carry it, so they're in Berlin, he hires a car for the two of them, where are they going, there's a side street, a narrow, dark street, she can't remember its name, there's a bell on the front of the house, what kind of place is this, should she wait downstairs, no, she's got to go up with him, she hesitates, doesn't know what to do, her heart hammering with fear, suddenly there's a dog, a big, brown St Bernard with a white patch on its forehead goes past, 'Come on,' the husband says, 'why are you staring at that animal', she doesn't know herself, the dog starts barking, whining, sidles up to her, sniffs at her and pants excitedly, starts to walk away and then comes back, jumps up at the husband and bares its teeth, or maybe it just seems that way, there's a woman at the door, she's no longer young, her face is all dried out beneath the makeup and pink blusher, she beckons him inside, seems to know him, he lashes out at the dog in his anger about the delay and pulls her inside, the painted lady curtsies reverently and gives a wide smile, a dim flight of stairs leading up, she's sick with fright now, there's a cramped room with a bed in it, the air's stuffy, 'Come on,' he says, his nostrils begin to quiver, he reaches for her with his fat arms, she tries to fend him off, she tries to scream, but he presses his blubbery lips to her ear and whispers, It's a fair bargain, you'll get a piece of gold each time, I'll buy you a nice dress and shoes and whatever you want, and if that isn't enough and you're very sweet, then you'll get two and then you'll be rich and later you'll marry a handsome man, as handsome as me, ha-ha! She's nearly suffocating, dizziness hits her, two pieces of gold each time, just one will be enough for the doctor, Mother will get well again, it won't last long, everything'll turn out fine, she can go home again, money, money, Mother, everything'll be fine. She has half fainted, he rips the clothes from her body, he heaves himself on top of her... 'Did you resist?' the lead judge asks, how was she to do that, 'it's a state of powerlessness, your honour,' I interrupt, my voice is hoarse and raw, I'm standing, I don't know why. 'Objection to the expert witness's intervention. This is a matter for the barrister,' Borges says. Yes, of course, but if he stays silent, if he doesn't say anything, this is a medical issue.

'It's a medical objection, your honours…'

'Objection,' Borges crows, red as a turkey, pounding his fist on the table; the lead judge waves his hand gently in the air.

'It's the defendant we want to hear from,' but now she has lost her composure, her voice wavers, she starts to sob, she can't remember what happened, he suddenly refused to keep his promise, he suddenly turned completely cold and turned over onto his other side, he'd got what he wanted and now it was done he lay there like a beast, it was all for nothing, all her giving and all her sacrifices, he'd cheated and lied to her, she was sullied, dishonoured, there was no money, no two pieces of gold, only misery, Mother would die, it was all over, and he was to blame, her virginity, it wasn't for love, it was for money, she'd become a hussy, through him, through that fat, red lump of flesh lying there, an infinite hatred overcame her, she hated herself, she hated him, everything went blurry before her eyes, she couldn't remember what happened next, suddenly the dog was in the room…

She says nothing more, despite their remonstrations, despite their encouragements, she remains stubbornly silent, she just sits there and weeps very quietly, her face a grimace, her lips trembling, she looks like a beaten child, she doesn't seem to hear anything now, just a picture in her mind's eye, a crime and a corpse, and this stifles her since it's all over now and what more is there to say, what does she care about the judges!

'Everything goes blurry before your eyes, you feel an infinite hatred, just then the dog turns up, it's striking…' the lead judge says, what is striking about it, 'so you claim it wasn't you but instead this mystical dog that went for the throat of the man beside you, what kind of dog was it, you told the investigating magistrate that you didn't recognize it, there was suddenly a noise outside the door and the handle was forced down, right?'

No, she keeps silent, no, she doesn't say another word, is she even listening, does she know where she is?

Next come the witnesses, the fat go-between, in a green dress, like a parrot, she's squashed her overspilling body into a corset, she has black eyes as round as marbles and a curly fringe, she speaks very quickly and excitedly, she has a lisp, spit trickles from her blubbery lips, that something like this should happen in *her* establishment, an honest establishment it is, only gentlemen frequent her establishment as the chief of police himself can confirm, she's an honest woman, she won't let anyone spread nasty rumours about her, she knew the landowner well, he often came to hers, if he was still alive he'd give her a glowing reference, but now that he's died in such a horrible fashion, the poor man!

She blows her nose fussily, there's laughter in the public gallery, the lead judge shifts restlessly on his seat, she's calm again at last, that tart strangled the nice gentleman, she saw it with her own eyes, how did she, wasn't the dog in there, see it with her own eyes?... Oh, the dog, yes, she couldn't really say for sure how the dog had appeared by the front door, snuffling around the girl the whole time, she has no idea what kind of dog it was, a brown fluffy St Bernard with a white patch on its forehead, and when the landowner slammed the door downstairs, it had stood there in the street, stayed there, staring up at the upstairs window, then she got scared, opened the door and the dog was inside and racing up the stairs, straight into the room where the two of them... and yes, she was right behind it, the door was already open, the dog ran straight towards her and out, and the landowner lying there naked on top of the bed, blue and with his throat gouged, she had to scream a lot and cry a lot, such a good man, and that tart was sitting motionless next to him in her blouse, she killed him, staring at her, all wild and fiery, and she got scared and ran to the police, didn't think twice!

She's allowed to step down from the stand, nodding her head regally, bowing, looking around triumphantly and dashing out, there's a momentary silence, then the lead judge says: 'There was clearly a fight between the victim and his murderer, they found traces of blood near the wound and on the floorboards beside the bed. The question is: what kind of blood is it, is it from the dog or the murder victim? If it really is dog's blood, which would be highly unlikely if this whole dog business were only a coincidental detail, it would prove that the dog was injured, that it had indeed been involved in a fight, and the dog had bitten the man's throat for reasons unknown. The expert witness has the floor.'

I stand up and go over to the judges' bench, with the sudden feeling that it's not me walking, that the table is moving towards me, the words rushing towards me, and I want to say something very different, my mouth, my lips move by themselves, as if against my will, and my voice says: 'Dog's blood, your honours, an examination has confirmed that it is dog's blood.'

The effect of these words is incredible, the public rises from the benches, there are incensed cries, the jury put their stunned heads together, the room is in uproar.

'Does the expert realize that he will be required to make a sworn statement,' Borges shouts over the noise, his voice cracking.

'I remind you of your duty and the weight of your statement,' the lead judge adds. 'The whole outcome of this trial may depend on it!'

'I know,' the voice inside my head says.

'Before the expert witness is sworn in, I would like to ask,' Borges crows, 'whether he has any relation with the defendant, it is possible, after all, and if so, I would doubt his credibility on such a key issue.'

'I am here in my capacity as a doctor,' my voice says. 'I submit a report. No personal issues are involved.'

'I have grounds to doubt the expert witness's credibility and sense of duty, I request the appointment of another expert and reject this one as biased.'

I lay into him, the blood surging into my brain, forgetting where I am. 'This gentleman…' I stammer, 'this gentleman dares to attack me here, this gentleman wormed his way into my family, claiming to be my friend, he…'

'This is not the place, doctor...'

'He's always on my tail, desperate to prove—'

'I ask the court to decide,' the barrister says.

The tribunal withdraws to deliberate, there's a short break, what's wrong with me, I smash the pane, I kick in the glass between him and me, I hate him when our paths cross, I club him over the head, I won't let them seize anything from me, not that either, not the girl either, none of this is any of my business, I'm just doing my duty, my duty?!

For a second I teeter, I feel very sick, everything starts dancing in front of my eyes, there's no time to think, the judges are back in their seats, the prosecutor's request has been rejected, they will not appoint a second expert, the lead judge insists that the court has complete confidence in my credentials and integrity, I take the stand for the defence, how I hate him, on Grete's account and on the girl's, it's all very mixed up, I put my finger on the cross, who, I do, me, my hand rises into the air, it isn't my hand, I can cut it off and throw it in the bucket, it has a life of its own, these words, my lips, a life of their own, I... I don't know who's speaking, there's a breathless silence in the court, I hear it and I hear my words dripping one by one from my mouth, and I see myself standing there, all alone, like in the grave, a voice from the grave, an oath from the grave, it seems as if I'm removed from myself, everything is in a fog.

I can't remember anything, Borges talks for a long time, and the barrister responds, the judges disappear again, a murmur goes around the courtroom, then they come back in, the lead judge makes a short speech, everything is fine, the girl's free, she staggers outside, Emmy, as she glides past I see her features, she looks at me, does she see me, me, the real me? Her face, white as snow and deadened, where's she going, oh follow her, she's free, thanks to me, thanks to me a person is *free*, what have I done, I'd like to smile, but my face is hard, almost frozen, I can't move a muscle any more.

At last I pull myself together, Borges walks past me, his eyes cold as steel, his head hunched between his shoulders like an evil bird, I hardly notice him, I walk through the dim corridors, down the steps, I feel alone, my body as heavy as a rock, I'm close to choking, I can't think, an unimaginable fatigue bears down on me, what life is this, I'm out in the street now, I go home, who knows where, suddenly a bright light stabs through the darkness: it's… the dog, a brown St Bernard with a white patch on its head, it's Nero, waiting over there on the other side of the street, coming towards me, barking, straight across the embankment, the dog, it's… how is this possible, what does it want from the girl, sniffing, smelling something on her, who, what… no one must see this or it's all over, plunged into an abyss, all of us, all of us, get away, quickly, run, round the corner, across the square, along the streets, the animal close behind, taking giant bounds, panting, its tongue out, now through the Tiergarten park, people stop and stare, a police officer turns around, I can't see now, I can't think now, I just run blindly, on and on, making for some objective, for some house or other, I'm at a front door, I rush up the stairs, I'm at the top, Grete, I'm in her arms.

'You're here, I was so anxious, and the dog's gone off again, it keeps running off, when you were in action too, for a whole day once, now we'll have to spend ages looking for it.'

'It'll be back soon… it's here already, in fact.'

'Should I lock it inside, did it try to bite you again?'

'No, no.'

'Did something happen? It's never allowed out again.'

'No. Has it got blood in its mouth? None of it matters anyway.'

'Was the girl acquitted?'

'Yes.'

'Did you play a part in that?'

'Yes.'

'Aren't you happy?'

'Sure.'

'Your face, though, there's been something off about you this whole time…'

Why's she asking, she shouldn't ask, no one should ask, I want to be left alone at last, I want to be able to lie quietly somewhere in this world, I'd like to shut my eyes and be dead and lie down there in the soil, it's a strange day, isn't it exactly a year since I came home, what has happened since, everything's against me, everything's pulling at me, someone is always on my tail, there's always someone lurking around, surrounding me, I can't get any peace, I can't make it feel right, I'm a speck of ash in the wind, I'm a fugitive from myself, I feel drawn towards an unknown destination, my centre of gravity is outside me, I keep grasping but my hands always come up empty, I can't settle, I'm always uncertain, I walk among people and they seem strange and foreign to me... Where, where are the hands that will finally hold me, where is the bottom I'm lowering my life towards, I'm swimming on the sea, I'm swimming on the wave, but my anchor is down in the deep, I've run aground in the blue darkness, and up top I'm dancing in the light.

'Hansi,' a voice says next to me, and that blue gaze stares at me out of two eyes, dazzled by love, 'Hansi,' laying her arm very quietly and gently around my neck, 'I want to ask you something, it's so hard when you shut your eyes and sit there all closed off, as if I wasn't here next to you, but it has to be now, I can't keep it to myself any more, it's impossible with grief, but with a happy event it is, you know, a happy event, something like this... why did you say before that I would never have your child, and now, now it's happened, I'm... now I'm carrying... your child... after all...'

I hear a sound, is it music, a voice comes and says something, I don't get it, I can't grasp it, it cannot be, it isn't possible, it's crazy, I'm suffocating, I'd like to shout out, I have a child, with her, inside her, I do, I do, I do... Grete!!

'What's the matter with you, you're frightening me, that face you're making... aren't you happy?'

This is what love can do, I, a human being now, this, this, across that, this is what love can do, across the abyss, across that there…

'Grete!'

'Oh!' she cries joyfully, her voice wavering and laughing and breaking and soaring like mine, 'Let go, your arms, I can't breathe, you're too strong, you're suffocating me…'

'For ever, for ever,' I stammer in stunned shock, I kiss her on the lips as a torrent of tears gushes from my eyes, everything's all right now, the sun's back after all, a happy event after all, now it's all over, nothing bad can happen now, she's built the bridge, right through the middle of everything, stronger than everything, now I'm part of the chain of the living, nothing bad can happen now?!

I enfold her frantically in my arms again, eyes asking hers hard and burning questions, she leans back, looks at me deeply and seriously, her lips are her answer.

Life begins now. Love overcomes life, it's all right, it's all right.

She's tired now, she needs to lie down, yes, it was all a bit much, I carry her to the sofa, she struggles, there's a charming smile on her lips, she doesn't want to sleep, I run my fingers over her hair, I put my hand over her eyelids, at last she yields, is she sleeping? Gently I pull back my hand, I sit beside her, I shut my eyes too, I'm happy, a melody ringing in my ear, I can't work out what it is, time trickles by, time trickles by inaudibly, you have to hold on to every second, the big clock ticks and ticks, now it winds up to strike, what's the time, there are four deep chimes, I count them automatically, it's as if it were totally outside me, then it slowly seeps into me, something starts to burn, yes, it's four o'clock, wasn't I meant to do something, Bussy, I have to go and see her, didn't I promise, it seems ages ago, but it was only yesterday, what do I care about her now, my place is here, but she'll be waiting, she has made herself nice and pinned up her locks, maybe her eyes are already peering out of the window, all dark and full of longing, her lips, and her head is slightly cocked, how I hate her, she should be thrown away like dirt, was she at the trial too, it doesn't matter, nothing matters, my place is here, my holy altar, I'm already here in that body, growing, hers and mine, we carry millions of us inside ourselves, and one of them is now growing in her womb and becoming a person, a different person, but still something that was me is now a different person, and I'm the same, made from two others, we should kneel down, we should doff our hats to every pregnant woman, this whole miracle is so close and so clear, we don't need a heaven, God is and always was on earth, heaven is always on earth. Now I must go, for the last time, I'll take Nero along, I'll be right back, by the time she wakes up I'll be back, she won't even notice I was gone.

In my mind I kiss her on the forehead, on her eyes and hands, I have second thoughts about leaving, my heart starts to pound again, why has all this restlessness returned, when I get back everything will be all right again, I inch my way across the floorboards on tiptoe, I open the door quietly, I look round one last time, I imprint the image of my sleeping wife deep on my soul, isn't she smiling, there's this longing inside me, an unspeakable pain all of a sudden, I'd like to stay, but eventually I tear myself away, shut the door, release the dog and I'm outside.

The rain has stopped now, a bright light is reflected in the odd puddle, I walk along the canal, the air is mild, young ducks are swimming on the water, still bearing the shape of the egg they hatched from, their downy feathers sticking out into the air, yellow, grey and brown, they chirrup and squeak in their mother's force field, paddling with their little feet in the great, dirty water, dunking their little beaks, catching something, in high spirits, a wide barge comes trundling towards them from the bridge, a man braces a long pole against the bottom and propels it forwards, his face glowing red in the sun, a young woman standing at the wheel in the back, a blue headscarf around her blonde hair, she calls out to the man, a thin stream of blue smoke rises from the cabin's small chimney, the ducklings veer off to the left, how do they know, where did they learn, they remind me of my amoeba at the laboratory, which has a body, sees, hears, eats, freezes, procreates and moves around, no eyes, no ears, no skin, no mouth and no heart, it's all of those together, it's all of those in one, it is life in all its tumult, that's how we should be, that's how I am in fact, but the others aren't, not even the women, only Grete, which is why she can do all of this, which is why she gets through it all, she lives and laughs and cries and loves, now she's lying on her couch dreaming, I need to hurry, why am I dawdling here, quick so I can get back home, I want to bring her a big bunch of flowers, flowers are the same, all alive with colours and fragrance, then the wind comes and pitches the seed through the air, and it lands somewhere and there they bloom again.

I'm walking quickly now, I'm short of time, I cross Lützowplatz, there's a flower shop on the corner, I go in, I buy three large tiger lilies, they're like three bloody spears in my hand, I'm at the underground, I walk through the stone-dead streets of Schöneberg, stop outside a house in Prager Strasse, I don't know this house, the dog creeps ahead up the stairs with its tail between its legs, looks back at me from every landing, there's something skulking about its behaviour, something spiteful, but maybe I'm only imagining it, outside the second-floor door it stops and wags its tail, I ring the bell, a maid opens, I'm in the hallway, she sees the dog and her expression turns embarrassed: 'Wouldn't it be better to leave the dog outside?'

'No, it's coming in.'

My voice is tetchy, what business is it of the maid's where the dog waits, if it makes a mess she has to clean it up, that's her job, she's trying to save herself the work, other people have to work too, hard and in unfair conditions, that's life, helping the groom muck out the stables, the wife's jealous and the husband takes her with him to the city, down a dark alley, he doesn't ask many questions and throws her onto a bed.

Work or starve, earn money or starve. We should pursue that: people are free, but what do they do with their freedom? Is everything all right now?

'You couldn't have got here any later,' Bussy says sulkily with her small, vicious mouth, 'but at least you didn't forget me completely and still thought about me a little bit.'

She reaches for the lilies I've held on to mechanically, unthinkingly, I didn't mean them for... they were for something else entirely, what did I want them for?

'What's wrong, don't you want to give them to me, it's as if you're going to hold on to them for ever,' she asks in astonishment.

'No, no, I just wanted, I... I'll look for a suitable holder, a vase...'

'Give them to me, I'll find one, or go and fetch the one from the bedroom over there, the crystal one with the silver stand, I hope you haven't forgotten everything, but be careful, I'll make some tea in the meantime, I assume you'd like a cup even if it won't compare to Grete's.'

I feel uneasy, a shadow falling on my soul, I hand her the flowers, they're dark, glowing arrows boring into Mary's heart, I turn hesitantly and take a few steps towards the door, suddenly she's right there behind me, her head close to mine, her hair touching my temple.

'Is that all I get in greeting?'

Her voice is dusky, deep and soft like her eyes, her pale head dotingly tilted to one side, she's wearing a bronze-coloured silk dress, her neck and shoulders are bare, her skin white and smooth, I bow my head, I kiss her on this cool, round ivory surface, her body quakes, she clasps my body with her white hands, her dark lips…

'Bite me hard with your white teeth!' she says, quaking hot. 'How I have longed for you!'

She's still holding the flowers, one lily catches on the table edge and snaps off, I notice a small, green-gold dot in her right eye, her hot breath strikes my face, suddenly she's completely foreign to me, I feel a strange revulsion, I draw my hands away from her body as if casually, what am I doing here, she hasn't noticed anything, adjusts her dress, gives me a melting, devoted look with those ever-moist eyes of hers, and whispers, 'The vase, one lily's a bit broken, it doesn't matter, my heart's the same, you take it in your hands and it's whole again.'

Opening the door, I'm in the next room, the air is sweet and perfumed, I feel dizzy, on the wall above the bed hangs a large oil painting, a naked girl with a book in her hand, on the white dressing table with the marble top there are little bottles, little boxes of all sizes and colours, ivory, porcelain and crystal, beside the large, oval mirror the vase twinkles, I reach out to take it down, I'm holding it carefully in my hands when there's a creaking behind me, I turn round and Nero has jumped up onto the bed, its front paws have found the wide counterpane to play with, the moist muzzle tears scrap after scrap off the precious lace trimming, in my shock I start towards the dog, but I stop, what am I doing in this bedroom, what am I hoping for, what does this woman want from me, it's absurd, she should leave me alone! Suddenly I'm filled with a strange hilarity: I'm standing in this bedroom, with a crystal vase in my hands, my dog's lying on the bed instead of me, picking contentedly at the blanket as if it were the finest of delicacies, as if it were a marrowbone, I have to laugh out loud, I can't control myself any longer, Nero has rolled up in the blanket and is looking out with round, amazed eyes and a dangling red tongue as if from under a nightcap, I fall into helpless fits of laughter, I forget everything as I stand there looking at the animal until tears leap from my eyes, I try to wipe them away with the back of my hand, the vase drops out of my hand, I try to catch it, it's in a thousand pieces.

Bussy is in the doorway, she sees me standing there among the broken glass, but even now I can't stifle my stunned laughter, she sees the dog in bed, sees her precious blanket torn to bits, the vase in pieces on the floor, all her poise is gone, she lunges at the dog, trying to grab the fabric from it, but the animal is tenacious, its jaws clamped shut, thinking maybe that this is a fun game, doesn't let go, she becomes more and more frantic, it's like a contest, like a mad dance, I'm still standing there laughing, her rage rises towards its climax, her face red as a cherry, no longer in control of herself, she screeches at me, 'You're laughing, you're standing there laughing! My blanket, my vase! This isn't the trenches!'

Her hair has come loose, she looks like a fury, Nero has jumped down from the bed now, some of the blanket is wound around the dog's left hind paw, it snaps at it with its jaws, bounding around in circles as if it's gone crazy, rolling onto its back with its legs in the air, now it's heading for the mirror, Bussy screams, and before I can stop it the whole table tips over with all the bottles, jars, powder, scissors, perfume, and shards of glass are sprayed onto the ground, a broad stream of green liquid smelling of ambergris and lavender oozes across the wooden floor.

The shocked animal pauses, then chases the oozing liquid with its nose to the floor; this is too much, I forget my laughter, make the most of the moment, tearing the remnants of the blanket from its jaws, I place these black, torn remnants in Bussy's hands.

She ignores my outstretched hand and bursts into tears, I feel sorry for her, she trembles as she pins up her hair, her dress is crumpled from the fight, her blouse open, she's weeping like a child, I go over to her, pull her hands gently away from her face, she's having none of it and slumps sobbing onto the bed. I wait for a while, stand there sheepishly among all the devastation, and yet I can't feel sad, Nero has crawled off into a corner and is looking at me, what kind of look is that, isn't it almost a laugh, why am I standing around here, there are such important things outside, things are very grave, it's very necessary that this ridiculous situation should end, patience deserts me, I step over to the edge of the bed, I grab her violently by the arm, my voice hard and horrible: 'I'm going now, I have to go.'

Suddenly she's up, she forgets the shattered vase, the torn lace, her bruised passion flares and pours out over me in a storm of insults: I'm a good-for-nothing scoundrel, a miserable cheat, the war has turned me into a ridiculous, mean, selfish brute, maybe I'm actually drunk, it wouldn't surprise her if I came to a lady while drunk, I'd never take that liberty with Grete, who knows what kind of strumpets I'm accustomed to, but she won't stand for it, definitely not, and now I can leave.

I turn on my heel and breathe out, determined to put an end to this and actually leave, but she must have taken this as an act, she bursts into tears again, stuffs her handkerchief into her mouth, jumps up, flings her arms passionately, hysterically around me, begs me not to abandon her, not to leave her all alone, she'll be herself again soon, she says she's been so anxious recently because I didn't answer her letters, she hated Grete so much, maybe I really did love her again, but that was ridiculous, such a pitiful woman compared to her... she looks ugly now, her makeup is smudged, you can see the tracks of her tears over the powder, her blouse is gaping open even more, one of her breasts is bared, I feel sick, I can't stand this cloying perfume smell any longer, I kiss her hand, I feel like adding something, but why, none of this is my concern now, I'm already at the door. Her sobbing suddenly stops, for a second she freezes, then with an awkward movement she pulls her open blouse together at the neck, an uncanny glint enters her eye, her soft lips become incredibly hard and narrow, she screams in a shrill voice, 'Go on then, go, I don't need you any more, I haven't needed you for a long time, go home all repentant to your sweet Grete or take any old tart, so this is the thanks I get for all my love, I know enough about you now, I've had enough anyway, if only my husband were alive, he'd tell you what's what, insulting a defenceless woman, my poor husband, you murdered him, Borges knows that too, if you hadn't gone away with me when he had his appendicitis thing, you would have operated on him and he'd be alive today, you wickedly violated your medical duty of care, as you know full well, I'm not to blame, you shouldn't have listened to me, my poor husband, my poor husband!'

I stare at her like a ghost, the blood draining from my cheeks, my body begins to shake, I can hardly keep upright, she notices the change in me, a dark triumph is reflected in her face, her anger and her hatred know no bounds now: 'Ha, now you're afraid of me, I'm cutting ties with you, Borges says that the business with the oath yesterday was just the same, Borges is a man of honour, he knows how to treat a woman, if he says something then it's true, he's much better than you, he's gentle and considerate, and he loves me, he's loved me for a long time, he confessed that to me, but you, get out of here, you and your beast of a dog… I waited for you for so long and now, now, I hate you, and you're going to pay!'

I'm numb, I can't hear anything, is this the same woman, the same person? Where's the beauty, the education, the elegance, the adoration, the love? All cosmetic, all a hoax, what am I doing here—out.

I don't look back, which is fine, she's ugly and cruel, I cross the living room, the tea still standing untouched on the table, the water heater steaming, there's tea and no one drinking it, it'll have to be cleared away again, it's actually very funny, it's all very funny, I wouldn't have thought Nero capable, where did he get the idea, he's like a human, he walks like me, we go up to a flat and now we're back out in the street, this has happened before, somewhere someone's standing at a window shouting, shouting on and on, and from the street someone comes, I come and walk up the stairs, always a different set of stairs, broad, bright and cheerful, then narrow ones that are cramped and dark and lead to poverty and death.

The front door snaps shut behind me, something's happened, something's been dealt with, that was a duty too, I have truly done my duty for once, and otherwise… I didn't otherwise? she hates me, she makes threats, what can she do, she's like a bedbug, wanting to bite me, crush her and bile will come out.

Now she has the lilies too, they weren't meant for her, she snapped them, as if they were bloodied, I need to watch out, they all need to watch out, they ought to have been white, lilies have to be white, they're the flowers of death.

I'm very gloomy, all my tension is gone, I'm free now, but I'm running on empty, what use is freedom on its own, you have to be able to force it to blossom, an acquittal doesn't yet spell happiness, I should have followed that maid, then I would know her way home, could accompany her and help her, help her get on… and I'd know the way.

Here I am again, roaming the streets, didn't I have a goal, wasn't everything all right again now, part of the chain of the living, yes, I want to go home, how long did you wait, four days looking out of the window and always waiting, finally putting the chair back without weeping, no, not a tear. Oh, I'm so full of longing, a mother has a child, one of the chain of the living, then the mother dies, and her voice searches and calls, searches and calls… until she's found her way.

It's already dark, twilight over the street, people streaming out of the houses, the offices, the shops, the first streetlamps light up, they're still small, yellow and round, as if shining for their own sake, all the light comes from below, from the silvery asphalt, while above the houses are in greyish-mauve shadow, and I feel as if I'm walking through an open tunnel, the air is mild, the air is tired, all the people stoop as they walk, now I'm at Potsdamer Platz, the signals change, electricity builds up and flows, I drift along, across the square, now I'm at the station, I go to the counter, I'm holding a ticket in my hand, I walk up the broad steps, lots of people here, they're carrying their belongings with them in their suitcases, their faces feverish, I walk alone, I'm isolated as if under a heavy cloche, the crowd builds up into a black circle by the gate, the barrier goes down, the crowd squeezes together as if through a bottleneck, they swear, they laugh, now they're free to walk on with their suitcases, dragging boxes and sticks and yet seeming to skip along the platform, I walk slowly with them, I stop at the carriage, I look at them uncomprehendingly as they awkwardly squeeze themselves and their luggage inside the carriage, shoulder first, then I slowly climb in myself to find people running, rushing, jostling inside the narrow corridor, at last, at long last they find their compartment, find their seat, they place the luggage in the overhead net, the window is wound down because some fresh air is needed after all of that and the air in here is stale and stifling and as musty as if it's been trapped here for thousands of years.

My seat is in the corner, by the window, Nero's lying by my feet, I let him jump up onto my seat, I go outside again, along the platform again, as if I'd forgotten something, I almost go back through the barrier, back into town, maybe I've just lost my way, I look at the large, dimly lit clock, five minutes to go, I look up at the great vault, there are isolated arcs of yellow light in this space, I look through the great arch leading out into the night, there are lights above and below, gold and red and green, I shut my eyes for a moment, there's a curious hum all around me, I hear the excited breath of the locomotive, a small cart with luggage on it rolls on its own straight past my feet with a brief, quiet, anxious tinkle, a voice somewhere calls out 'Cakes' and 'Siesta, lights out' like a Mohammedan's call to prayer, two minutes to go, the masses converge on the train, a call of 'All aboard', the windows are wound down, the heads of those departing look down, while those staying behind crane their necks, words cross like a bridge, I stand alone beside my window, who is there to speak to me, I have nothing to say to anyone, the train pulls away, gliding out of the station, drawing the waving, weeping, shouting people alongside it for a while, creeping out of a kind of dark shell now, it's out now, slender and ponderous, jolting, swaying, passing through several switches in the tracks, the gold and red lights stretching out, two brightly lit suburban stations sliding past, a suburban train at the platform over there soon abandoning its attempt to compete; through the glass I see the people in the illuminated compartments, the small, rattling locomotive, golden sparks flying through the red glow around the top of its chimney, it's dark at last, a few last lights flash past, the route is clear, leading into the night, into the distance.

    I go back to my seat, Nero lies down under the bench again, I soon close my eyes, it's like a living room, a living room racing through the landscape, it's hot and the round electric light blazes down from the ceiling.

    Sitting opposite me is a girl, lank blonde hair framing her pale, tired face, she's wearing a windcheater, her delicate feet thrust into clumpy, brown boots, next to her an elderly woman, on a grey cushion, a teacher perhaps, her lined cheeks inhaling air, she has awkwardly put on some spectacles and is absorbed in a book, of the three men one has removed his jacket, his waistcoat's open, he's swapped his boots for slippers and his grey woollen socks are showing.

Then the conductor comes for his checks: one man's getting out after only three hours, another and the old lady around midnight. I sit for a while with my head out of the window looking at the dark countryside, the cold stream of air against my right cheek, I pull my head inside, I feel a peculiar inner restlessness, the man in the corner has lit a fat cigar, pungent smoke rises blue and heavy to the ceiling, the man next to him has folded his hands over his belly and seems to have already fallen asleep, I clamber over six legs, push back the glass door and am out in the corridor again, I walk in the opposite direction to the one the train is travelling in, peeking through the windows into the compartments at the people sitting on the other side of the glass, as dreamlike as objects in a shop window, I hear muffled voices, the next one's already dark, sleep having settled over them, I go back to my compartment, the girl has got up from her seat and is leaning out of the window, I join her, we talk, she has ten days' holiday, she's going to the mountains, we stare out together, we talk about the stars above us, we talk about her job, her mother, of destinies and people still awake out there under a lonely light in the villages, we are no longer in the compartment, we're hanging our heads out into the night and have forgotten the people behind us, we glide on and on, stations loop past with their lights, another train, the lights dance before our eyes like a golden snake, then there's nothing but the broad plain again and our night-time conversation.

It's long past midnight, we've grown tired, apart from us there's only one other person left in the compartment, he's taken off his shoes and is lying long and stiff on the wooden bench, we pull up the window, we're suddenly back in the warmth and the room, I invite her to lie down, she hesitates, looks at me with translucent blue eyes, I'm in real pain, who does she remind me of, I lay my blanket over the bench for her and sit down in the corner, she's lying next to me, her head resting on my lap, a small curl of her blonde hair has come loose, her eyes are shut, her long, dark lashes twitch, a smile has come over her pale features, this is all so familiar, this is all so familiar, I can't sleep, my eyes are stinging, there's a dull pain in the front of my head, the wood of the wall jabs into my temple, there are the muffled sounds of a conversation in the next compartment, the man in the corner is snoring, his mouth hanging open, his nose pointed and strangely white, on my lap is the blonde, sleeping, smiling head of an unknown girl, it's completely silent, the countryside speeding past outside, a fly crawling slowly across the forehead of the man over there.

I must have finally fallen asleep too, now it's bright in the compartment, outside a hilly landscape is still asleep under bluish fog, my hand's resting on something soft now—it's Nero, the dog must have jumped down from the bench opposite during the night, what made it suddenly come to me, doesn't it hate me any more; 'Nero,' I call very quietly, half dreaming still, its nose is on my knee, its tail wags, it looks at me quizzically and sadly, its tongue laps warmly at my hands. Moved, I stroke its coat, almost happy now, the animal loves me again, why does it love me now when it hated me before, I shut my eyes again, I sleep deeply and soundly.

We're close to our destination, I help the girl get her suitcase down from the luggage net, she looks ugly now and grey, the man pulls on his shoes over his grey socks, the train stops, we're in the station. I go out through the gate and up Kaiserstrasse to Rossmarkt, the dog close and seemingly fearful at my heel, I turn right into the narrow alleys, it's as if something is pulling me along, I'm walking blind, everything seems so familiar to me and yet so infinitely strange, I don't actually want to go there, I have to go somewhere entirely different, she's lying on her couch asleep, before she wakes up I'll be there, I'll be with her.

Now I'm outside the old church, I'm walking around in circles, I've seen these houses before, earlier, maybe I should go back to the station, there's no point walking around here in the narrow alleys, the dog looks tired too, it's walking slower and eventually lags behind, it looks in all directions, an old maid is sitting at a street corner, eating her meagre breakfast in the sunshine, and it stops in front of her, wagging its tail, she breaks into a smile, her small, old hands stroke its brown coat, she tears a chunk off the bread she's eating with difficulty and holds it out to the dog, which greedily snaps it up and lies down in front of her market stall with its head on its paws, the old woman bends down and it's as if the two of them are having a conversation, I whistle, it doesn't move, I have to go back and get it, laid out on the table are soap, cigarettes, colourful glasses, and I buy a few cigarettes from the old woman, she curtsies and giggles and says, 'A ribbon for that lovely dog perhaps, green or brown', I take them as well, both of them, I pay, Nero gets up reluctantly, stretches in the sun, our wanderings begin all over again, I'm on the Zeil, the first shoppers appear, I go into a few stores, examine what they have, then come back out again, turn right again, down a small side street there's a bakery, I go inside, the little bell on the door tinkles, silvery and bright and on and on, fresh rolls lie there in a basket, cakes and tarts on smooth, white porcelain. I reach over the counter, pick up a bun and tear it apart.

'Customers aren't allowed to serve themselves,' says the small, curly-haired salesman with important, arched eyebrows.

'Take off the apron before you come out into the shop,' I say, 'and the buns are much too soggy again.'

The boy's uncertain for a second, first he's embarrassed, then he blushes and finally he stands up defiantly.

'It's not allowed, the boss said no one's allowed to reach over the counter and take things.'

I feel calmer, suddenly I have to smile, I ask politely for a piece of cake, I find it good and tasty, I ask, 'Is your current boss good to you, has he made many changes?'

The boy is starting to trust me; no, the boss has left everything the way it was, he wanted only to add an extension out back, next year maybe, but otherwise he was stingy, the old boss spent a lot more freely, he also paid him higher wages, but he was ambitious and had a nasty temper, oh, sometimes...

'But you liked him?'

Very much, he'd been dead for a year now, did I know him? No, no, and now it's fine, and how much is the cake?

I pay, giving him three times the price, he stares at me in amazement, I'm already back outside again, back out in the street, I shut my eyes, it seems as if someone's calling my name, I walk along a bit with my eyes shut, it turns cool, I've stepped out of the sun, I'm standing in a gateway, there's an old, winding wooden staircase leading up to my left, I whistle to the dog, it isn't there, I go back out, it's lying in the sunshine again, I call its name, it squirms and won't be moved, should I beat it, why, it wants to lie in the sun, it should lie in the sun, I go back into the shade, I go up the creaking stairs, it feels as if there's a dark black cloth over my soul, I can hardly breathe, I'm filled with endless fear, I can't take another step, I stand there motionless in the darkness, the wooden door looms in front of me, it's off the latch, I don't dare knock, after a long time I hold my ear to the door, something's going on inside, something's happening inside, I've got to hurry, but my strength is gone, I hear moaning and breathing and in between quiet weeping, a man's deep voice is speaking in a grave, matter-of-fact tone, I hear a patter of water, then there's a break, no sound except the moaning, I'm about to step back, I'm not a thief, turn around and walk away, when the door opens inwards, a man steps out with a small briefcase, adjusts his glasses and says half under his breath over his shoulder: 'I'm going to the clinic now, if anything happens, call for me! And be nice and sensible and avoid any excitement, any excitement at all!'

There's no answer, he goes down the stairs, walks past me, I'm standing in the shadows so he can't have seen me, I feel like screaming, I mustn't hesitate any longer, I have to go in there, someone's lying on the couch in there waiting for me, with her eyes closed, and when she wakes up, I'll be there, I'll be standing next to her and she won't have noticed I was even gone.

I'm standing in the doorway, it's a small, bright room, a small attic room, the light dazzles me, I've been standing in the dark for so long, and for the first few seconds I can't see anything, I just hear a quiet cry and straight afterwards a dull thud, I cross to the corner with big, heavy strides, the girl's lying there on the floor, groaning and sprawling against the chair, I crouch down beside her, she opens her eyes, her whole body's trembling, her wide eyes stare at me in horror.

'Not now,' she mumbles, almost inaudibly, squirming in terror, 'you can't do anything to me now, I was acquitted, the verdict is final, it can't be reversed now, you might have got it wrong, it's possible of course, you must have got it wrong, but now, now... I need all my strength, if in here... when she's well again, just come back, nothing will matter then, I'll do anything you want then, I'll make any statement you want, then I can die for all I care, not now though, not now, I'll confess to anything, it's too horrible, I hated him so much, my hands reached for his neck all by themselves, I squeezed until his eyes were bulging, harder and harder, harder and harder, I bit into his throat, deeper and deeper, my hands dug into his skin, blood flowed out, his breath slurping more and more, the muscles of his neck went taut, I didn't let go until he was still, I didn't know what I was doing. That dog, how would I know what dog it was, kept sniffing at me, already down at the gate, and then in the room suddenly until it went out again timidly, maybe it was the devil, maybe... So now you know everything, I'm a murderer, you saved me, do whatever you want with me, nothing matters to me, life has no meaning for me any more, but now I have to live, I'm not ready yet, now I have to live, I have to live...'

'Emmy,' I whisper breathlessly in her ear, 'Emmy, what are you saying, that's not why I've come, everything's all right now, I've just come... Mother's in there, right?'

She gets up, her eyes frozen, she looks at me timidly side on, her face completely white, she's holding the handkerchief in front of her mouth, her voice quivers: 'You don't want to hurt me, no, you're kind to me, you helped me, why did you help me, why are you being so kind to me?'

'Mother's in there, right?'

'Mother, yes, she's very sick, I don't know, the doctor was here before, he says, he said a Latin word for it, he... you want to see her, you want... how did you know...'

'She called me.'

'Mother? When? Who did she get to call you?'

'A long time ago, a long time, over a year ago,' I say and shut my eyes again.

She takes a step back, her face full of fresh terror, horror and fear are written on her features, she doesn't believe me.

'Don't toy with us... God can't punish me like this, if you hold anything sacred, you're a doctor, you were good to me. Help me, save me, why were you so kind to me and now you want to abandon me?'

'Come,' I say and in place of an answer I take her cold hand. On the threshold I stop, I put my hand on her shoulder, my voice wavers from shock, and I can hardly get a word out for emotion.

'Emmy,' I say, 'trust me, believe, don't ask now, and if there's nothing to be done, if she really does... die...'

I can't go on, my voice breaks off, I wait for an answer, I can't see her face now, I hardly know if she's still standing next to me, I go in there, one step at a time, I close the door behind me like the stone lid of a grave, I'm in the middle of the room now, the small window's open, a hurdy gurdy's playing, on the floor are gold ringlets of sun, they're right in my path, I have to walk over them with my profane feet, it's like sacrilege, I'm on holy ground, over there is the bed, from over there in the corner comes breathing, muffled and heavy breathing, a lung is fighting, a heart is agonizing, someone is dying...

Mother...

Yes, now I'm by the bed, I kneel down, the world stops here, my hands are on the white blanket, my hands clasp hers, oh, her white hair and that pale face, hands that searched, hair that has turned grey from waiting, worry and want!

I take the pillow and place it under the wheezing chest, I raise up the poor, small, groaning body until it's lying comfortably and softly, I wet the cloth a little so that it rests cool on the wrinkled face, I'm a doctor, I'm familiar with suffering and death, I know the ways and means to soothe and comfort.

Now she opens her eyes, the eyelids roll up, swing up towards the ceiling, whirr around in a daze, past me, over me, without seeing me, without seeing me...

I bend down close to her, I grab the pillow tightly in both hands, my face next to her ear.

'Mother,' I sob, my voice failing, tears running hot and wild over my mouth and cheeks, 'Mother, I'm here, hear me, see me, you didn't wait for nothing, I was away for so long, I've been looking for you for so long, it was very hard, everything was against me, I'm not human any more, everything was always foggy, I was always torn apart, I don't even know myself, no one's with me, I'm always on my own, you know, I'm only ever a shadow of myself and I can't see... but you, you're here, you were always here, I was always on my way to you, you just slept for so long. You've lain here and I was gone for a moment, but now I'm home, now I'm here, now you must open your eyes and hear me because I'm back, just hear me one more time, one last time, one last time...'

I cover her hands with kisses, her forehead with kisses, it's cool and moist, I put my ear to her heart, it's ticking only very quietly and barely audibly, it feels like no more than a fluttering now, soon it'll be silent, up above the fight goes on, breathing hard and sorely, a rattling buzz in her chest, her mouth's open, its right corner drooping, the skin over her pointed cheekbones is caving in, her nose is growing cool and sharp, I don't give up, I gather all my strength, she has to hear me: Mother, Mother, Mother... the eyes open again, they beam into mine, there's a sparkle in them, they look through my body, seeing me, the real me, there's a twitch of the lips, her hand tries to rise towards me, touch and stroke my hair, but halfway there it sinks back down, the breathing pauses, my heart stops, there's a horrible silence, her chest rises one last time in a terrible spasm, her mouth contorts as if in final disgust, the eyes sink down, her face turns white and cold, it's over.

I stand there and listen, where is she now, a person just before, Mother, won't she move one last time, hands, lips, say another word… it's all over, all the warmth is gone, all the life is gone, a cold body lying there that used to be something, it's over.

Why am I still standing here, what am I doing here, a stranger, an unknown old woman is lying there, cold and dead, I no longer know what brought me here, I'm in a small, old, ugly room, sun and air coming in from outside, somewhere out in the street a kid is shouting, why might that be, I go over to the window, I look down at the people, down below Nero is lying in the sun, boys standing around him, the hurdy-gurdy man puts the organ and the monkey on his back and moves on to the next house, I close the windows, I let down the white blind, the room is grey and in shadow now, it's completely silent, I go over to the bed again, there's nothing else, just a poor, old woman I could no longer help.

'How is she?' comes an anxious whispered question from the next room, 'is there any hope, do you think—'

'She just died,' I say. 'You need to call the doctor who treated the patient.'

With a scream she's in the room, with a scream she crumples down next to the bed, I stand there impassively, it's sad when people die, but it happens to us all.

I lift the weeping woman to her feet, she hangs there in my arms, completely broken, I run my fingers over her hair mechanically—how unhappy humans are, how unhappy I am too!

What should I do, I let go of her, I put a few banknotes on top of the cold fireplace, I don't look back, I go out of the door and into the sunshine.

I whistle for Nero, the dog jumps up happily, wagging its tail, there's sunshine, there's sunshine, but I can't feel it, the people who come towards me look past me, no one knows where I was, not one that I have already been with a dead person this early in the day, they're all very busy, why are they in such a hurry, one day they'll be lying in a room, and the ringlets of sun on the floor will fade into shadow.

It's all quiet inside me, there's no grief and no happiness, no sunshine and no suffering, I'm just infinitely tired, it's all for nothing, it was all for nothing, while I'm walking along here an old woman is lying on a white bed up in a small room, I'd like to be lying somewhere too, someone collapses in tears next to me and kneels beside my bed, but a stranger will be standing there, saying, it's sad when people die, but it happens to us all.

Where am I going, the tracks behind me vanish, the voice behind me is gone, behind me there's silence, the rope has torn free of the ground and I'm floating, floating back and forth, I don't want anything now, I'm not looking for anything now, I just want a piece of land to rest in, some earth to give me peaceful shade…

Westwards, westwards, where am I heading, I'm sitting in a train again, the border's far behind us, where to, those are French uniforms, French villages, the compartment is full of people, a foreign language strikes my ear, the window's open, I see nothing, I hear nothing, people get on and off, we're moving through a small valley along a river, we travel past green hills, through broad fields, through picturesque small towns… I see nothing, I sit in my corner as if it's a grave, I walk through large underground halls, the ceiling's low and oppressive, it's a dugout, the shells come, earth above us, the lonely footstep echoes back off the damp, stone walls, there's a dim blue glow, the light falling tired and shattered through a few cracks in the wall, there are the dead, they're all dead, I grope my way from one coffin to the next, I knock on each lid, I pore over every name, I'm carrying a small candle in my hand, the small flame trembles and flickers, an icy chill comes off the walls, I can't read the names, some letters are missing, some of them have crumbled with time, they're overgrown with green, blurred and faded, I have no time to stop, it goes on, on and on without a break, my feet get sore, my ears deaf from the same footstep over and over again, my robe peels off, now I'm naked, my skin is layer upon layer of scabs and bark, they too fall away, brain too, muscles and nerves, diaphragm and gut, only the heart is left twitching, a small, red flame, looking and bowing, keeps looking, keeps beating, just wanting to rest, finally rest but can't and is tired, so very tired…

Am I already asleep, in the middle of the day? The window's open, I don't look out, all the splendour of the countryside, the splendour of the flourishing soil, the splendour of the blessed fields races past me, I don't see it, it isn't for me, others will reap, others have sown, I don't envy them, I don't envy anyone, I used to, but now that's over, everyone bears their own fate, no one is happy, we shouldn't tempt the dead either, there's a human will, it rears up, it wants to jump out of its box, go beyond itself, it wants to break its fate, it wants to be God, it wants to soar over the earth, over misery and bodies and coffins... and yet it falls back, imprisoned by itself, and cannot escape itself, it rises up against him, it snatches at him with its hands, he tumbles backwards until he suffocates.

Am I already asleep, I have such a desire and I don't know what for, I want to wake up, I want to see my own life all the way to the end, I've jumped into a river and now I've got to swim until it spits me out again, we're all sitting in this train, life slides past like this scenery, with hills, fields, towns and people, but we've just been sitting in our seats, sitting in our corners and staring straight ahead, the same wood wearing our backs sore, the same bench opposite us, the same other person, the same other mask sitting next to us, and only once does the train stop, finally we can get up, we can get off, and the journey is over.

Where am I, darkness is already falling outside, the countryside has changed, half-collapsed churches, devastated villages and ruins pass by, here a trench ploughs through the land, here lie wire and rotten boards and wood, here blood flowed, here raged murder, hell and madness, here men sat like moles beneath the soil, watched and mangled one another, here there are no more trees, the leaves have fallen off and withered, the trunks are bare and black, no houses not buried under screams, fate and affliction here, here the air shook with the horror of exploding shells, somewhere here I too sat, who—me... who, what, where am I, is the train stopping, is the journey over?

Yes, I walk across land, across bare earth, yes, I climb the hillsides, this is Verdun, these are the heights of Douaumont, I leave the bombed-out town, there's scaffolding everywhere, building is going on everywhere, there are new outside walls, new inside walls, they're still yellow and bare, I don't see any of it, it's all the same to me, all I hear is the whimpering around this town, the ring of fire around this town, all I hear is the whimpering of the dead; the world burned here, millions were charred to the bone and bled dry here, our brothers lie here, Europe lies here, humanity lies here, I'm here, I lie here, my life lies here, graves lie here, graves and graves, cross beside cross, earth beside earth, black crosses for the Germans, white crosses for the French, black stones, white stones, who controls this board game, who moved the pieces, move after move, we can swap the pieces, who is the god who manipulates our lives—against us. There's a road leading up the mountain, we drove this way with our cannons, water came to the thirsting here and turned to blood, life marched up here and marched back as death, now I'm on top of the hills, there's no grass growing here now, there's no greenery and no bushes, everything's grey, everything has been razed to the ground, no wind blows, no breeze stirs, it is silent, it is silent for ever, down below is Fleury, down below was Fleury, down below was a village, were white houses, was life, warmth, fate, love, where's Fleury, a sign says *Fleury*; this is Fleury now, graves and earth and dust, up above is Douaumont, up on the hill above lies mangled cement, mangled earth, armoured turrets, mangled iron and steel; death blazed here, right and left, Germans shot here and Frenchmen shot here, Germans lie here and Frenchmen lie here, there is no war, people lie here, there is no enemy, there are no states, there are no destinies, no differences, no officers, no rich, no workers and commoners; we are naked, naked, we are naked, mortal men.

It's getting dark, I stand by the memorial up on the hillside, a lion pierced by an arrow gasps its heavy, marble life out into the sand, something dark is poking out of the earth, I bend down, it's brittle and hard, I pull it out, it's a scrap of leather, a haversack strap, it's stained with old dry blood, a year has passed and there's still blood here, I throw it away, the dog leaps after it, ah the dog, it barks and darts around, it has completely changed, running around in the train before, from one seat to another, out into the corridor, over to the window, nose in the air, sniffing, restless, beside itself, then back at heel, pleading with its eyes, wagging its tail, it jumps back up onto the bench, presses its trembling body tight to mine, tongue panting, it lays its head flat on my lap, its eyes are closed, it looks as if it's crying, it lets out a quiet whimper,

I stroke it, the dog presses its muzzle between my arm and my body. Now though it acts as if it barely knows me, I've put it on the lead, it drags me through trenches, across fields, over fences and wire, nose to the ground, it moans and whines and barks, it doesn't heed my calls, snaps, there's foam around its mouth, I can no longer hold it, with a jerk it breaks free, jumps in the air, races away, the lead trailing along behind it, snagging on things, now it disappears into a trench, there's water in the bottom, the dog sprays its way through it, is already far in the distance near Douaumont, I have to make a detour, I can't see it any more.

The sun's gone, it's slowly getting dark, it's slowly getting cold, I'm still working my way breathlessly along the hillsides, like the dog I have my eye on the ground, I'm crawling more than walking, what am I looking for, am I only chasing the animal, am I looking for my dog, am I looking for a person or maybe even for myself, I can hardly see anything, I can hardly make out anything now, I stumble over stubble, over boards and wire, there's something warm and sticky on my foot, I think it's blood, it's still warm, it can't be anyone else's, I've scratched my foot, is it my blood, I keep going, I'm totally alone among the dead, it's totally dark now, I'm scared, I'm scared as one of the living, I feel a cold and terrible fear, but I can't leave, I've got to find my dog, why did it run away, the silence grows ever more awful, my throat feels constricted, I see the long, blue, echoing corridor again, as if in a fever I see the coffins again, I knock on each of them, little white threads stretch out on all sides, white cobweb feet, they bend upwards, the coffins lift off the ground, noiselessly they get into line, they begin to circle around me, from all sides they come up out of the depths, the earth cracks open like a thousand white wounds, it seeps towards me, forming a procession, it stretches from horizon to horizon, Verdun is burning, Verdun is burning, and my heart is skipping in the darkness, my little flame skips and twitches around every coffin, it dances and glows, two dots glow in the night, I stumble, my cold hand touches the ground, feels something warm and trembling and soft, the two lights turn, start to dance, begin to move, I'm nearly going mad, I want to scream… It's the dog, it's Nero, it's a warm creature, a warm, breathing body, it's lying on the ground, I can only see its eyes, I touch the dog's body, I feel the earth around it, there should be a wire to the right here, barbed-wire entanglements, behind that is the listening post, a small, narrow protruding trench, it's all very familiar to me, there was a telephone hanging under the board, it always made a very high-pitched, lilting ticking sound, when the wind came from the other side we could hear the gramophone until it was shot to bits, it must have a hole in it now, a piece of metal with a round hole in it, and maybe it's lying around here, I was in this post once before, something happened here, was it yesterday, it was in the daytime, but there were noises over there, cheers came drifting over, and me, I was lonely, I was cold, wind blowing like now, two eyes looking the same way, glowing out of the emptiness, wouldn't close, they were human eyes, I wanted to get out of the darkness, out of the night, out of the misery, out of the war, out of the squalor, out of the loneliness and death… I want to go back to the music, I want to go back among humans, I've gone astray, I've gone backwards, there's no rewinding, there's no stopping, not life and not death either, it's cold, and I want to be in the warm, two eyes are glowing at me, but they're the eyes of a dog, bodies around me, thousands of them in the earth, but I want to be with living people, I want to touch blood, I want to feel warmth, I want to get out of here, I want to go back to the light, I want to live… Grete! Grete! Come on, Nero, don't stare at me, dog, there's nothing here, why won't you move away, you're coming with me, I'm your master and that's an order, are you laughing, trying to bite, what are you doing there, it's only earth, they're only bones, it's only dust, there used to be someone lying there, now it's cold, a ghost is on the prowl, what's dead is dead, who'll thank you for your loyalty, are you coming, I throw stones at you, you don't budge, what is it, what keeps staring, I'm afraid, I'm going nuts, I'm alone here with a mad animal, the animal is lying on top of me, lying on my chest, maybe it's already dead, it can die for all I care, it can lie here until Judgement Day, it can…

I walk fast, I'm running now, I trip over crops and fling myself to my feet again, my foot's hurting, where's the path, if I can't find it, if I have to stay here through the night, between dread and death, the whimpering is still coming from over there, it sounds like a child wailing, someone shouting for help, the dead are shouting for help, the dead want to reach the light, that terrible sound again, the dog, only it knows what's wrong with me, it knows everything better than I do, I won't see it again, that was its last cry, maybe it's been torn apart, maybe only its soul is sitting over there by the corpse wailing, and the dog comes after all, walking behind me, always walking behind me... No, I don't want this, it's got to stay here, it's got to stay with the dead, maybe it's actually dead, maybe I'm actually dead, a ghost crawling between the crosses, a human being, an animal... Run and keep running, away from here, to find some humans, human eyes, humans, Grete, the path, white gravel, the stone lion, everything's stone, everything's dead, I too am dead, now around the bend, now downhill, the town, lights, now voices, bells, music, houses, a road... I'm saved...

How long was I gone, is it hours, was it days, is she still lying on the couch, is she still sleeping, I should never have left, maybe she hasn't noticed, for sure she hasn't, still sleeping, and I'm there, I hold her hand quietly, the clock ticks, she opens her eyes, a smile crosses her lips, 'I slept for a long time, were you sitting there the whole time?'... 'Yes,' I'll lie, 'yes, it's warm in the room, I held your hand, I was waiting the whole time for your eyes to open, maybe my thoughts wandered once, that's possible, ideas come into your mind if you sit like this for hours, but yes, you were always there, yes, I was sitting here the whole time and holding your hand and watching over your sleep, and I'll never go away, never, because I love you, Grete, because I love you.'

Now I'm outside the front door, it's been one long horror and nightmare, everything's fine, I will rest in your eyes, I will learn to smile, as purely as silently as she does, I will… have a child, my God, did I forget that, is it possible to forget that, if something's happened to her, there was no one with her, if she has got up and fallen over now, or if someone has come, some person crossed the threshold, a life crossed the threshold… In one bound I'm upstairs, I pull the bell, it quivers and gives a shrill ring, I put my ear to the door, I think I can hear voices, women shouting, anxious running around, what's going on, I don't know that voice, Grete, no, a man, the pane of glass, now I kick it in, I yank the bell until it comes off, isn't anyone going to open up, I bang on the door with my fist, at last there are footsteps, slow and heavy, the bolt is pulled back, those were a man's steps, where's the old woman, the door opens and there is… Borges, his face is white, his eyes glare at me full of scorn, he's blocking my view, Bussy's voice screeches from inside, 'Let him in if he *wants*', I grab him by the arm, I don't know what's going on, I can't form a thought, eventually I say absently, 'Why are you standing here, how did you get in here, what are you doing here, where is… Grete?'

'Inside.'

'Well, get out of my way then,' I gasp, 'who let you—'

'You're not coming in here, this woman belongs to me now, I'll be able to… protect her from criminals.'

I reel backwards, a chill runs through me, I look at him very calmly, like something unknown, for the first time, my voice trembling imperceptibly, I ask, 'Where's Grete, you're nothing to me, I don't know you, where's Grete?'

'Inside,' he says again, and his shoulder seems to spasm, 'we know everything, Bussy told us everything, you left her cruelly, you're a liar, you violated your oath as a doctor, you're a murderer, just as I thought back then, I went looking for evidence, Bussy loves me, she told me everything, they'll deal with you as you deserve.'

My hand lunges at his chest and he recoils a step.

'Don't try anything, it's no good, I'm not involved with Bussy, I put on a whole act of loving her to unmask you, I know everything now, that's enough, I told Grete, she belongs to me, she knows everything, she has fainted from the shock, she's bleeding, the child, she doesn't want to raise a criminal, if she dies then all the better, she has nothing in common with murderers and perjurers.'

Did I yell, did blood spurt from my eyeballs, was a hammer lying there or was it just a plank, I can't remember, it rested heavy in my hand, my hand grasped it, swung it hot and high through the air and smashed him straight in the face, he crashed to the floorboards, it was a terrible fall, blood flowed, running from his left eye, from his left ear, I stepped over him, I'm by the door, I push it open with a jolt, I'm in the room, Bussy is standing there pale with fear, screaming, what do I care about Bussy, but she's lying there on the bed, Grete is lying there, is she dead, her lips are white, her eyes are fixed and staring and white and gaping at me, what are they looking at, what is it about my hand, I drop the instrument I'm still holding, it clatters to the floor, I fall to my knees beside the bed, with her last strength she raises a shaking, transparent hand, she shields herself, tries to push me back, no, no…

'Grete,' I shout, out of control, 'it's all true, I can't help it, I'm not me, you know, I didn't do it, I'm not a murderer, not then, it was the other man then, what do I care, he needs to clear that up with himself, I love only you, I killed him for you, you're my wife, I took his name, and I only killed now because I have his name, because he's a murderer, not me, he's a perjurer, not me, he's a criminal, not me, but I love you, beyond everything else, I love you, I do, from the core of my being, with all my soul, with all my heart, don't push me away, don't leave me, not now, now you know my secret, I wasn't brave enough to tell you, I was a coward, now it's too late, now a man is dead, it just happened, I'm innocent, how could such a creature understand, but you'll understand, you have to understand, the dog knew from the start, ask the dog, it realized everything, all by itself, now it too is dead, lying somewhere in the dark, it forgives me too, it won't hate me either, but you, you have to live, I've already lost so much, I always wanted, desperately wanted to escape from myself, it didn't work, it's unfair, I could scream, why are the officer and that other guy rich and I'm a proletarian, no, I'm both, I'm an educated man, I'm a doctor, I claim my destiny, I claim my happiness, but it's full of suffering like this, full of torment like this, they're both the same, it's no use, what good did it do me, we have our lives, it doesn't matter what the situation is, we take it and live it out, *it's only ever the hours, only ever a person*, Grete, I won't leave you, I can't leave you, not now, not ever!'

Her blood ran and ran, two lives sinking as one, I was a doctor, could maybe have stopped it, but I had no strength left, I simply kept an eye on all her facial expressions to see if she still loved me, if she believed me, if she forgave me, her hand jerked towards me once, it all suddenly seemed so familiar to me, a hand had done this once before, I'd been this happy once before for a short time, what was supposed to happen now, her face grew paler and paler, the sparkle in her eye faded and faded, then came a very gentle trembling, then it was all over. I walked out of the door, I didn't look back, Bussy stood ashen-faced to one side and tried to hold me back, another woman stood beside another bed, but she was a stranger to me, I can hardly remember her voice...

So here I am, your honours, do what you want with me, it's all the same, demand whatever you want, just... name, passport, yes, I must have it here with me, it's here in this pocket, here inside the jacket, over my heart, why do you want it, why don't you believe me, here it is, there, you have it, it's the only thing I still have to give away, and it's… what's happening to me, what am I doing, isn't my hair white, is my skin turning yellow, I feel so tired, I can't stand up any more, it feels as if stones are dragging me down, a hundredweight of them, I can't breathe, it's… earth, I'm breathing in earth, I'm lying under the earth, I'm choking, help me please, I'm ancient, I'm not human any more, I'm not even here, next to me are crosses, crosses, the earth is black, shells are flying, I've been lying here for so long… in the earth, I am at peace now, I am at peace.

# LOOKING BACK

*Peter Flamm, whose real name was Erich Mosse, which he Americanized as Eric P. Mosse after arriving in the United States, travelled to Germany in 1959 to attend a major International PEN conference in Frankfurt and give a talk with the title 'Fiction in the Scientific Age'. His return to his former homeland prompted him to examine his own past as an author and a Jew and gave rise to the following self-critical review.*

I F I REMEMBER RIGHTLY, it was the permanently rather embittered and moralistic Ibsen who wrote: 'To live is to battle the demons inside oneself. To write is to sit in judgement over oneself.'

I don't see any clearly delineated boundaries in this definition. Writer or not, each of us is doomed—or blessed—to battle the demonic bubbles that rise up from the dark, seething waters of our unconscious. Freud expressed this better, in cooler and more sober terms: the critical 'ego' is engaged in a constant battle with the archaic emotional legacy of the 'id'. It is the author's prerogative to record this process. It is an inventory of the soul, not judgement day. The medieval whiff of guilt and redemption lingered on in the literary noses of the nineteenth century, and now it is time to consider some disinfection. The archives of the state prosecutor and the permanent dust lying on our exterior and interior tribunals need a better system of ventilation. As authors, we want to be able to look around and stop condemning, accusing and prosecuting. The machinery of moral evaluation was once invented *ad majorem dei gloriam*; but now we are God. It is a self-destructive mire—sterile, arrogant and debilitating. As authors, we escape from all of that. We try to look *sub specie aeternitatis* at the planetary system, of which we and the Earth happen to be a part. Must we always live with value judgements?

It would appear salutary and fruitful to pause for a while every so often in this hectic marathon and take stock of our state of mind. This break will not harm the naïve joy of our existence; on the contrary, it will enhance it. Asking 'why' is more than just a pleasant way to pass the time. We enjoy playing, but the delights of our childhood must give way to the fact that we were not pleased to leave behind the dramatic bronze doors to a paradise of entirely vegetative existence. It is no good: we, like any plant, must grow up.

The question of why I do not live in the Federal Republic of Germany has never seriously bothered the cells of my cerebral cortex. I am too caught up in the present nature of my life as it is. That may be a good thing. Maybe I cannot afford to live hand in hand with the past. It was too painful, and the hand was too easily paralysed. I forget what I wish to forget. I have called this a constructive and healthy neurosis. We cannot carry all our ballast around with us all the time. We throw what bothers us overboard—as far as possible.

Once more, then: *je n'accuse personne*! Psychiatry has taught me to understand, not to judge.

So, for this special occasion I shall make contact with my reliable rubbish collection service and dig the faded nostalgic films out of the increasingly grimy cardboard box. I shall run them on the projector of my mind—and here they are:

I was born a Jew, but I felt more German than many other Germans. I spoke German, I wrote German, I felt German. The brother I so admired was killed in the First World War while serving as a Bavarian lieutenant at Verdun. He had volunteered to lead his company on a hopeless patrol when none of his fellow Germans wanted to go with him. In his pocket they found a letter with the words: 'We do not want to have read our German classics for nothing.' No, it wasn't for nothing. He died for the idea of Germany.

My father was the first eminent Jewish lawyer to become a higher regional court judge. His appointment cost the justice minister his job. My father was supposed to be elevated to the supreme court. The new minister confessed cynically and publicly that he had no intention of sharing his predecessor's fate. However, if my father would get baptized… 'Gladly,' the privy councillor replied, 'but only as a Catholic.' The minister got the message. My father received an honorary doctorate and became a full honorary university professor, a city councillor and a city elder of Berlin. This was a giant, many-layered plaster on a wound I didn't want to see.

My uncle founded the *Berliner Tageblatt*. It had nothing to do with Judaism; it was a newspaper of German enlightened democratic values and fought for international understanding and peace. Later, when I was older, I worked under my pseudonym Peter Flamm for the *Tageblatt* and Ullstein and all the leading democratic newspapers and magazines. The shadow over my childhood had lifted. An aristocratic young man and a fellow pupil of mine at high school once called me a 'Jewboy'. I punched him in his white, doughy face, but I am sure that this educational distinction didn't stop him from later becoming an Obergruppenführer or something similar in the Nazi hierarchy. It didn't affect me any more than that. I was top of my class in German essay-writing and Christian religious education. I later worked as a doctor, and my patients were my friends. I published four novels, and my readers and even a few critics liked them. I didn't agree with them and asked my friend Max Scheler about the best way to learn how the human clock ticks. He said, Read Freud. So I read Freud. My friend was right: you have to know something about psychological x-rays before you can paint other pictures. And that's how I got into psychiatry and psychoanalysis. It helped me, and I helped others. I continued to write. Several plays staged in half a dozen theatres. I became a dramaturge in Frankfurt and Hamburg and Bremen, and a theatre director in Kassel. I gave speeches and debated and trumpeted the broadcasts of my heart and head on every German broadcaster. Until the morning when everything came crashing down in a single day. Where death was at my heels and I had to sneak out of Germany through the back door as a beaten and humiliated man with no money, no homeland, no friends and no language. I was a Prussian—can you tell my allegiance?

Fade out. End of part one. Ladies and gentlemen, please do not leave your seats. This intermission will, by necessity, be a short one. If you should wish to go outside and get cold, I do not pretend to be able to warm you up again. In the meantime, for your entertainment, here is the compère. The Americans call him a 'commentator'. This is what he has to say: 'I was a Prussian—can you tell my allegiance?' But we know that already, and why repeat something when no one understands—when no one wants to understand. It's better that we proceed straight to part two. I predicted that the intermission would be brief. I predicted so many things, but how many have ears to hear?

Fade in. This is the Voice of America. This is a welcome to free America. This is unexpected generosity. A readiness to make sacrifices and provide human kindness. This is the cold dollarland of reality where everything is a race and everything is immediately exaggerated to bombastic levels. Where technology with steel, glass, cement and electronics still cannot stifle the silent voices of religious irrationality. Here are the skyscrapers and social scabies. The same obsession underpins them both. The same compulsive, almost utopian urge for boundless mobility, which can just as well reach for the sky as rush—at breath-taking speed—to eradicate all the world's social and ethical scrapes. It is life itself, in all its nuances and contradictions. Tough, unsentimental, materialist, yet not at all cold. Calculating, yet naïve. Often small-minded, yet with a haphazard idealism verging on the quixotic.

New York is home to the United Nations, housed in a glasshouse. Very tall and airy. And woe betide anyone who throws stones here! Their culinary representatives are spread throughout the city, no less tasty and often just as unappetizing as those sitting inside the glasshouse: Russian, Scandinavian, Italian, French, Chinese, Japanese and Javanese—and your stomach is your battlefield.

All of this is my world. I walk through the bare streets and the dressed-up parks. I go to the harbour, and there lie the giant hulks of the steamers that brought me here across the ocean and take me back every summer—for short visits. I stand looking at the shop windows on Fifth Avenue, and my eyes buy everything my wife and child might desire. My child is beautiful and full of laughter. Before she was even born, I saved her from Germany's moral collapse, and now she walks with me through the streets of New York, through the parks where squirrels cross your path. She has her arm tucked under mine, and she possesses the rare gift of pleasing God and humans alike. She has an American husband who looks as if he was drawn by Albrecht Dürer; she speaks in addition to her literary English a language that sounds almost like German but is more of a Middle High German. (She calls me 'mein sueßer Bursche'—'my sweet fellow'.) She is full of idiosyncratically creative ideas and not just for her publishing house, and her joyous happiness is plain for all to see. And that is my happiness—how could it not be?

My wife sits with me in an apartment high above the park. She has been with me through all the misery and all the triumph. Through every window we look out into the open air; it's like being in a lovely, comfortable lighthouse. Except that down below is not the ocean but greenery. In autumn it turns red, purple, orange and lemon-yellow, and beyond are the grey and blue silhouettes of the high-rise buildings. In the evenings they stand out blackly against the flaming sunset, and then out come the thousand lights and a bleeding moon with a buzzing plane below it, arriving from Germany or some other place on Earth. Magic stares at you wherever you look—in this, the most real of all cities.

It is the same with everything else. A man has a dream of tearing down all the crumbling, sickly tenements and building a gigantic cultural centre in their stead: modern buildings with trees and plants all around it, for theatre and music, dance and science—and an entire university is to be built alongside. It is under construction. Not all the money has been raised yet, but it will soon be there: Washington and the state of New York and New York City, and all their citizens who can afford it, are throwing their dollars into the hat, and within two years the greatest concentration of art, science and beauty, teaching institutions and experimental theatres, opera and concert halls the world has ever seen will be standing there.

All of that is my world. I am with my friends and my foes, and I never want to give them up. I came here with nothing. I lost everything in that one single hour—and with my own hands I built everything anew for myself. The clear fullness of this new language is now my language, my new riches. I wasn't born into it, and, unfortunately, I still need someone to set me right. I am still caught between two chairs and two continents. I haven't been broken by this weight. My horizon is wider and more open. I have become stronger—and more grateful.

Fade out. There is a lot more I could say, but that's enough for now. We don't need any more films. Here's the compère again. He would like to add a small detail:

After all of this I came back to Germany a few times—as an American. I took part in the International PEN Club congress in Frankfurt and made my short speech in English. My friends attacked me mercilessly. Wasn't I a German writer? Yes, but I was a member of the American delegation. Pensively I contemplated the ruins of the Kaiser Wilhelm Memorial Church in Berlin. I wondered why this old Willy had to be immortalized when there were newer and better ones. I heard about the argument over what kind of new architecture was to be added. Maybe three entrances and three wings, it occurred to me: one Catholic in design, one Protestant and one Jewish. Those are the mixtures of styles that we admire in our medieval cathedrals. A harmonious merger of them would have been hugely symbolic, worthy of a new era and a new spirit—if it really exists.

I visited the other ruins: the human ruins and the others. The manner of their 'reconstruction' wasn't always to my taste. I admire the capacity to rebound, the constructive ambition, the sincere opposition to rearmament. But I observed with horror that former Nazis were in positions of great power, and alongside an accusing, sensitive, talented and well-intentioned younger generation, I saw uncompromising, arrogant and noisy agitation to block this development. I was touched by the taste and ability and creative intellectual approach of a theatre scene that I could not relate to the cultural destruction that had gone before. And I couldn't forget the gesture of the young man who threw his arms around me because my radio broadcast had 'shaken him so much'. I appreciated his emotion, but while his body was so close to mine, I could not shake one thought out of my mind: *And who did you kill?*

I didn't want to say all those things. I am doing my best to see the light alongside the shade. Every light casts a shadow. I am speaking and writing this with a kind of fervent shame. My old love refuses to die: my love for the German landscape and language. For a culture of the past that has remained my present. For a life that felt closely bound to friends I admired and liked. Sometimes I go to one of the German beer halls in New York. I laugh at the stuffiness, at the noise and the beer and the delicious bratwursts. And I laugh at myself. At my ridiculous nostalgia and a small, sentimental sadness. Then I walk through these streets by night again and through this noise full of so many wonders, and I wish goodnight to every star. Let's go home! Where is home, though? You can't go home again.

## AVAILABLE AND COMING SOON FROM PUSHKIN PRESS

Pushkin Press was founded in 1997, and publishes novels, essays, memoirs, children's books—everything from timeless classics to the urgent and contemporary.

Our books represent exciting, high-quality writing from around the world: we publish some of the twentieth century's most widely acclaimed, brilliant authors such as Stefan Zweig, Yasushi Inoue, Teffi, Antal Szerb, Gerard Reve and Elsa Morante, as well as compelling and award-winning contemporary writers, including Dorthe Nors, Edith Pearlman, Perumal Murugan, Ayelet Gundar-Goshen and Chigozie Obioma.

Pushkin Press publishes the world's best stories, to be read and read again. To discover more, visit www.pushkinpress.com.

**THE PASSENGER**
ULRICH ALEXANDER BOSCHWITZ

**TENDER IS THE FLESH**
**NINETEEN CLAWS AND A BLACK BIRD**
**THE UNWORTHY**
AGUSTINA BAZTERRICA

**SOLENOID**
MIRCEA CĂRTĂRESCU

**THE WIZARD OF THE KREMLIN**
GIULIANO DA EMPOLI

**AT NIGHT ALL BLOOD IS BLACK**
**BEYOND THE DOOR OF NO RETURN**
DAVID DIOP

**WHEN WE CEASE TO UNDERSTAND THE WORLD**
**THE MANIAC**
BENJAMÍN LABATUT

**NO PLACE TO LAY ONE'S HEAD**
FRANÇOISE FRENKEL

**FORBIDDEN NOTEBOOK**
ALBA DE CÉSPEDES

**COLLECTED WORKS: A NOVEL**
LYDIA SANDGREN

**MY MEN**
VICTORIA KIELLAND

**AS RICH AS THE KING**
ABIGAIL ASSOR

**LAND OF SNOW AND ASHES**
PETRA RAUTIAINEN

**LUCKY BREAKS**
YEVGENIA BELORUSETS

**THE WOLF HUNT**
AYELET GUNDAR-GOSHEN

**MISS ICELAND**
AUDUR AVA ÓLAFSDÓTTIR

**MIRROR, SHOULDER, SIGNAL**
DORTHE NORS

**THE WONDERS**
ELENA MEDEL

**GROWN UPS**
MARIE AUBERT

**LEARNING TO TALK TO PLANTS**
MARTA ORRIOLS

**THE RABBIT BACK LITERATURE SOCIETY**
PASI ILMARI JÄÄSKELÄINEN

**BINOCULAR VISION**
EDITH PEARLMAN

**MY BROTHER**
KARIN SMIRNOFF

**ISLAND**
SIRI RANVA HJELM JACOBSEN

**ARTURO'S ISLAND**
ELSA MORANTE

**PYRE**
PERUMAL MURUGAN

**RED DOG**
WILLEM ANKER

**AN UNTOUCHED HOUSE**
WILLEM FREDERIK HERMANS

**WILL**
JEROEN OLYSLAEGERS

**MY CAT YUGOSLAVIA**
PAJTIM STATOVCI

**BEAUTY IS A WOUND**
EKA KURNIAWAN

**BONITA AVENUE**
PETER BUWALDA

**IN THE BEGINNING WAS THE SEA**
TOMÁS GONZÁLEZ